More Lost Memories

Short Stories by

Teel McClanahan III

Modern Evil Press
Phoenix

First Edition

This is a work of fiction. Names, characters, places, entities and incidents either are the product of the author's imagination or are used fictitiously. Any resemblance to actual events, locales, organizations, or persons, living or dead, is entirely coincidental and beyond the intent of either the author or the publisher.

Published by Modern Evil Press, Phoenix, AZ

Printed in the United States of America

ISBN-13: 978-1-934516-04-1

Library of Congress Control Number: 2008944068

– for love lost, and for love found –

Preface

This book, *More Lost Memories*, is a companion to my novel, *Forget What You Can't Remember*. As I was writing that novel, I kept finding that certain interesting things that popped up there had to go unwritten (or be set aside) since they weren't relevant to the story of that book.

What happened to the two guys who were supposed to be running the zombie survival course? What would the experience of a mixed martial arts competition be like for someone with an amazing sense of smell? What are the stories behind Fantastician's other encounters? What about the details of Lance's restaurant? And, what did Brady work on after the stunning conclusion of the novel?

Answers to all these questions, along with a story which further connects the events of *Lost and Not Found* with *Forget What You Can't Remember* by bringing the main characters of one book into the setting of the other, can be found in *More Lost Memories*. Delve deeper. Find out more. Enjoy.

-Teel McClanahan III

Contents

Pay Attention
-A Zombie Story-

The Sergeant walked away with Lorraine by his side. Mary's eyes were stuck in a shocked stare, liquid leaking silently from them and down her face as she watched the object of her desire slip away with her best friend.

"You heard the man! Find shelter! Arm yourselves! This is a test, and you will be graded on your performance!"

The crowd of trainees scattered, searching the woods, running across fields, looking for the cabins that would protect them from the undead. Lance and Brady ran off in the same direction. Most of the others kept to groups of two or three. Mary didn't move, she just kept looking in the direction the Sergeant had gone in, as though frozen.

"I'm sorry about that." One of the instructors approached her, speaking in a familiar tone. "I was sure he'd go for you. He really does have a thing for red heads."

Mary's eyes snapped across to meet his eyes. Her head, her body, her streaming tears remained as they were. Her lip trembled, but she did not speak.

"Why did you bring her along, anyway? She hardly looks fit to survive a full zombie survival training course." His tone was gruff, even though deep down he was glad to see the Sergeant distracted and it didn't matter to him which woman it was doing the distracting. "If you'd gone off with him, she'd be the one stuck out here by herself. Did you want her to be zombie bait, or just to have to put out for protection?"

Mary sniffled. There were only a couple of trainees still in sight. The other instructor was waiting, a few feet away, bruised and impatient. Mary's hands rose to her face and futilely wiped away her tears. Her tears didn't stop. Being accused of wanting her best friend murdered hadn't helped.

"Look, we're being watched, so you're going to have to participate. Stephen," he addressed the other instructor, "did you happen to notice if any of the cabins didn't have someone headed to it?"

"Hard to say. No one was headed for eleven, but two groups are gonna hit the outer wall if they stay on a straight course. No way of knowing where they'll end up after that."

"Wait," Mary's voice was hoarse and accusatory, "I thought you told me your name was Steven."

"It is."

"But you just called him Steven."

"No, I called him Stephen. He's Stephen with a 'ph' and I'm Steven with a 'v'." Stephen finally crossed the distance to where Mary was still standing frozen in place. "Stephen, this is Mary, the woman I was telling you about. Mary, this is Stephen. He'll be assisting me with running the new facility out West."

Stephen reached out a hand, but Mary did not take it and after a moment he let it fall back to his side. "Pleased to meet you, Mary."

"Okay, so, do you see that boulder over there, kinda shaped like a bear?" Mary's eyes moved to the boulder. "Cabin eleven is about ten minutes into the forest if you walk a straight path past that boulder. There are plenty of big knives in the kitchenette and there should be a hunting rifle in one of the closets." Steven glanced at his watch. "Someone will be checking in at each cabin in fifteen minutes, so get there and get armed before they show up. Remember, zombies can't use language, so don't open the door for anyone who doesn't. Now go!"

Mary's hands reached up and halfheartedly wiped another face full of tears away. She took a deep breath. She gave Steven a look that she hoped expressed that she couldn't do this without him. She ran off in the direction of the boulder and was quickly out of sight amongst the trees.

"She's going to need a lot of help to survive this thing, herself."

"I thought she'd be protected by the Sergeant. Now I'm going to have to try to keep her safe without compromising her training and run the entire camp for the rest of the trainees at the same time. What a headache."

"Well, at least the Sergeant won't be around to muck things up for us."

"That's what you think. The other instructors are loyal to him, not us. If he wants us to run into snags, he doesn't have to do it himself."

"So what was the point of the girl?"

"He won't be breathing down our necks is the point. I wish he'd gone for Mary, at least then I'd know he'd be satisfied, and more likely to go easy on us at the end of this. That girl can take anything the Sergeant can dish out."

"Then why are you worried about her surviving training?"

"In the bedroom. I meant she could take anything he could dish out in the bedroom."

. • ● ● . .

"Which is why you never want to punch a zombie in the mouth." Stephen was explaining to the assembled trainees that there wasn't really any difference between being bit on the hand and breaking the skin on your knuckles against the lipless grin of a contagious zombie. "Don't use your own body as a weapon. Pick something up. It doesn't matter whether it's a stone or a hunk of wood or a fire axe, as long as you're not coming into direct contact with the undead. Most of you seemed to find suitable weapons in your cabins. Why don't you share a few of your discoveries with the group?"

"I found a crow bar," said Brady, lifting it up so everyone could see it.

"Good. A crow bar can be an excellent blunt instrument. It has good heft, so you can usually crush a skull with a good swing, and the curved end makes a good handle. Just be careful not to turn it around and get the curved end stuck in someone's head, or you'll find yourself disarmed. What else?"

"I found a set of golf clubs," another trainee announced, brandishing a huge driver overhead.

"Golf clubs are better than your bare hands, but be careful with them; their effective range is pretty small. If zombies get too close you'll just hit them with the shaft and even if it doesn't break the club, it won't be enough to kill 'em. Swinging a golf club around in the air may seem intimidating to you, but remember that zombies aren't thinking creatures. They won't be afraid, they'll just keep coming, and unless you can crush their skull with the head of the club, you'll be dropping it to switch to another weapon once they get in closer. What else?"

"I've got a shotgun!" A huge, muscle-bound hulk of a man grunted, proud.

"That's alright, but we're really looking for blunt instruments. You can swing a shotgun and get a pretty good hit, but if you can keep from damaging it in close combat, you won't have to worry about trying to repair it later. We'll get into making your own ammunition and weapon repairs later this week, and you'll really see what I mean. You run out of shells for that shotgun and you put it away and you get out a blade or a blunt instrument or you pick something up off the ground if you have to, but unless it's life or death, you're better off using anything but your shotgun to bash skulls with. What else?"

"I'm pretty happy with the sledge hammer I've got here." Lance hefted the eight pound sledge up over his head. "I've split a lot of firewood and pounded enough tent pegs that I'm quite accurate with it."

"Excellent choice for you, then. That size hammer has a good reach, and more than enough heft to crush a skull or knock a few zombies back so you have time to get them one at a time. The only advantage a big, heavy pipe has over the hammer," and Stephen indicated the pipe in another student's hands, "is that its weight distribution makes it easier to handle. If you have the practice necessary to handle it, choose the hammer. For the rest of you, choose something simple, with an even weight distribution, like a two by four, a pipe, a branch, or a table leg. Long enough that your fingers aren't in biting range and heavy or sturdy enough that you can crush skulls or knock heads off entirely."

"What about knives?"

"Big blades are great, and after lunch you'll all be getting hands-on time with the machetes you'll be taking home with you. Machetes, swords, Bat'leths and other long, sharp blades are excellent for beheading zombies. Large kitchen knives and hunting knives can be effective, if you have time to sever the head, or if you can stab backward through the eyes and into the brain. Don't try to defend yourself with knives six inches and shorter. Even if you manage to stab a zombie in the eye, you won't be able to do enough brain damage to kill it. Generally though, if you're getting close enough to stab the thing in the eyes, you're close enough to get bit, so anything shorter than a sword should be used as a last line of defense."

"What about an axe? An axe is like a blade on a stick."

"An axe can be very effective against zombies, as can a scythe if you know how to handle it. Try to focus on fast, clean decapitation with an axe. I know it's gonna be tempting to drive that thing into a zombie's skull, but like the wrong end of a crowbar or like an axe going into a stubborn log, it could get stuck. If it does, you're either distracted, you're disarmed, or you're dead." Stephen was getting tired of having to run all the classes by himself, without Steven's help or the Sergeant's guidance. Nearly a dozen of the regular staff had been sent along with the supply convoy to the new camp being set up out West, and those who remained were barely able to keep up with the regular schedule. "Now, it's time for lunch. We've removed the rations from all but two of the cabins, and only one of you knows which two. You have two hours. You can fight, you can cooperate, you can go hungry, I don't care, and no one will stop you. Remember that in the end, you won't know when or where your next meal will come from, or who you can trust. All you can be certain of is that death is waiting around every corner. Now move, if you want to eat!"

A few people ran off together in the same direction, then almost everyone else followed. Stephen knew the one who had been told where the food was had led the first group away, and that he was the greediest bastard in the class. Stephen also knew that the closer of the two cabins also had a few zombies. Every time, for every class, they hinted on the first day that it would be a good idea to hide some food, in the event of a zombie outbreak, preferably a little in every room you could find yourself trapped in. Every time, they did the same thing, stocking every cabin before anyone arrived, then removing it from all but two cabins the second morning, and trying to show them a little something about preparedness and about teamwork. Once again, Stephen thought as he walked briskly toward Steven's accommodations, not a single trainee had both thought to hide food somewhere in their cabin and remembered doing so when presented with this challenge. Yet another lesson he would have to explain to them all personally, if Steven didn't get himself back to work. Stephen threw open the door when he reached it, forcibly letting himself in and making a show of his anger. Steven and Mary were on the couch.

"You're supposed to be out there with me, Steven! You're the one who's supposed to be running the new camp, and this is supposed to be your final test. Why am I the one out there earning your grade?"

Mary screamed into her ball gag, and let out little more than a muffled squeal. Steven stepped backward out of and off of her naked body, glistening with sweat and flush with pain and excitement. She moved to cover herself, to turn away, to hide her nakedness from the intruder, but there was nothing at arms' reach to cover herself with, not even a throw pillow. She ended up folding her handcuffed arms in front of her, crossing her legs, and lowering her head in shame.

"Has there been a problem?" Steven walked confidently nude across the room and pulled a beer from the fridge. "You want one?"

"I'm working, and you should be, too!"

Steven closed the refrigerator door with a shrug. "Look, I know the Sergeant hasn't left his cabin since he went in there with... Uhh..."

"Lorraine," muttered Mary unintelligibly through her ball gag.

"Yeah, with Lorraine. I don't know what it is she's been doing to him that Mary wouldn't have done, but I doubt we'll see him again any time soon."

"That's not the point." Stephen offered his coat to Mary, politely keeping his gaze on Steven as she covered herself up. "You know we're short staffed, right now, what with the transfer going on. And this is a full house, Steven. It's more students than one instructor was meant to handle. Between those two facts, people's lives could be at risk out there, while you're in here..." Stephen didn't finish, out of courtesy to Mary.

"What I do in here is none of your business, Stephen, and if you aren't capable of picking up the slack then I might need to start looking for someone else to be my number two at the new camp."

"Look, can you at least make it to machete training after lunch, today? Some of these people are going to need a pretty close eye on them just to be sure they don't chop off their own fingers." The sound of distant gun shots pierced the air.

"I think they found the zombies you left to guard their lunches. Is it still the brute carrying the shotgun?" Stephen nodded. "How many do you suppose will survive 'till machete training? With that guy waving his boom stick around?"

"Less than would have made it if I'd had your help last night. I wasn't going to try to take the thing away from him by myself."

"You think I would have helped? That guy could take both of us in an instant." Steven was already finishing his beer, and walking back to get another. "I'd bet that before we send him home he rips a zombie's head off with his bare hands, just because he can."

"I'd rather bet that he tries using the shotgun as a blunt instrument and ends up blowing his own head off."

"Sure, but he'd take the zombie with him."

Another couple of shots could be heard in the distance. "I better go check on 'em. Can I count on you? Machete training, two hours?" Steven only nodded as he popped the top off another cold bottle of beer, and Stephen trusted him and went back out the door he'd left standing wide open on his way in. Steven looked at Mary looking curled up and ashamed on his couch, and a devilish grin grew across his face.

. • ● ● • .

Steven had thought it was Stephen at the door again, letting himself in. He had thought it would be another way to dominate, control, and degrade Mary to force her to be seen as she was. After the better part of a week had been spent alternately beating Mary, fucking Mary, and ignoring Stephen's requests for assistance, Steven had forgotten about just about everything beyond the walls of his cabin. It didn't occur to him that the sound of the door opening and someone coming in without knocking hadn't been accompanied by more shouting and yelling until he felt cold fingers on his shoulder and sharp teeth soon after.

Naked, armed only with a calf-skin flogger, Steven was no match for the two zombies that had caught him totally unawares. As Mary watched them approach, she had tried to warn him, tried to shout out, to indicate with her eyes and with the look on her face that Steven should turn around, but between the ball gag and his trance-like mental state, he didn't get the message. A distinct change in the magnitude of the fear in her eyes and on her face ought to have registered with him, even after seeing pain and fear in her for so long, when she went from sub-space to raw horror and terror at their imminent demise. Still, his incomprehension had given Mary an extra moment to react, as both zombies paused to consume his flesh one mouthful at a time.

She felt sure it would not be moment enough to escape. Mary was laying on her back upon Steven's dining room table, naked except for the ropes that held her arms and legs to the table and the ball gag in her mouth. She was spread-eagled. Her arms were flat on the table, her wrists tied by short pieces of rope to the tops of two legs of it. Her spread knees were bent down over the opposite edge of the table, her ankles and calves secured to the other two legs in three places each. She had spent nearly an hour struggling in vain against her bonds before the pair of loose zombies had come through Steven's unlocked front door and begun to eat him alive. When she saw that the man she had been trusting to protect her had failed so quickly and completely, the table finally gave in to her adrenaline-fueled strength.

The table gave in, but it did not give up, and she was not freed. Her legs, straining forward, backward, forward, backward, forward, backward, inching the table across the floor, finally managed to snap its legs from its top. The legs broke inward, sliding in under the table, and the table and the weight of her whole body came down with it. She had been straining with her entire body, and luckily her toes had been included; their being curled back allowed part of the weight of the blow to roll over the balls of her feet and reduce the force that ended up crushing down on her knees. Her hands were still tied, and her body was still spread out across the table's surface, only now it was wedged diagonally between the crooks of her knees and the ropes burning her wrists.

The zombies were still only a few feet away. Mary could smell their unmistakable odor, she could see Steven's blood pooling on the floor, and she knew she needed to keep her wits about her. Using the strength of her legs and her abs alone, Mary pulled hard against the table, lifting it up off the floor behind her. Then, when she had it as high as she could get it, her body nearly vertical, she slammed her full weight backward against it.

She heard something crack.

Slowly, painfully, she pulled herself up and up and up again, not quite as far as before. Again, she slammed backward with as much force as she could find.

Another cracking sound.

A third time she strained against the ropes holding her, against her past which had brought her there and got her in that position, and against the weariness not just of the last few moments but of the last week altogether. The zombies seemed already to be losing interest in the cooling flesh of Mary's recently deceased lover. She pushed back hard, one more time, unsure if she would be able to pull herself up again if this blow was insufficient.

A louder crack, then almost a boom, and finally she was falling backward as the other two legs of the table gave out one at a time behind her.

It was a stroke of luck that the legs gave out one before the other, because it pulled the table down to the left rather than straight back. She was able to twist her legs out from under the table to the right as it came down instead of hyper-extending her knees and possibly tearing her own legs apart with the force that a straight fall might have had. Her wrists were burned, strained, and pained, and her calves were still tied to table legs, but at least she was free.

She crawled on her hands and knees across the floor away from the zombies, finding her hand land on the thick wooden table leg that had been holding her captive only an instant earlier. As the first of the zombies lurched her way, she lifted the leg up like a club. Mary was surprised she couldn't feel its weight and didn't have to strain to lift it. As the first of the zombies came within range, she swung the table leg in a wide arc, beaning it. The zombie fell to the ground. She slammed the leg, her captor transformed thus into the savior Steven could now never be for her, again and again against the thing's skull, crushing and nearly pulverizing its brains against the floor.

The second zombie didn't seem to mind the reduced competition for her warm, bare flesh, and approached hungrily. Mary tried to stand. She even tried using the blood and bone-encrusted table leg as a prop or crutch to help her up. Mary couldn't stand. The table legs tied to her legs were like terrible stilts, and she quickly saw that she would not be able to stand or to run until she was able to remove them. The zombie moaned. She swung at it, hit it, and was disappointed to see that it did not hit the floor as easily as its companion. She swung again. Her blow hit more solidly. She heard bone breaking and saw the zombie's motion cease and limbs go limp before gravity could get a grip on him. Mary pounded mercilessly on the second zombie's already destroyed head for several more minutes, until her strength gave out. She collapsed beside the dead bodies of the undead she had been avoiding all week, pulling the gag out of her mouth, finally able to take a deep breath.

She cried.

She sobbed.

She wept.

She wailed.

But not for long.

Mary knew it would not be long before Steven's dead, partially eaten body began again to stir. She began working to untie her legs. She began thinking about whether she would have time to get dressed before he woke up. She was pretty sure she wouldn't be able to kill him as easily as she'd killed the other two; she hadn't known the other two. She hadn't fucked the other two. They were merely monsters. They were easy. She had her first leg free.

"There's been a zombie outbreak--!" Stephen came shouting into Steven's cabin yet again without knocking, but stopped short when he saw the death and destruction laid out before him.

"I know," Mary said without looking up from the tangled knots holding her second leg.

"What happened here?" Stephen was trying not to look at Mary's naked, bruised and battered, zombie-blood splattered body, but between it and the broken table, dead zombies, and Steven, he couldn't help but stare.

"You just said. Zombie outbreak, right?" Mary's second leg was free, and she was up and stiffly walking into the bedroom to get something to wear. "Do I have time to take a shower, or are more coming this way?"

"I don't think you understand. These zombies didn't break out. Those two were from a training exercise, earlier." Stephen threw a dish towel -the only thing he could find laying around- over Steven's exposed genitals and then looked away again. "I came to tell Steven that there was a real zombie outbreak. Near Denver. The Sergeant says we've got to get everyone trained and ready to go before we all head to Denver at Noon."

"Fine. Plenty of time to take a shower, then," and Mary went into Steven's bathroom with a handful of clothes and a fresh towel and shut the door behind her. Stephen heard the water running before he could run out the front door on his way to alert the other trainees.

. • ● ● • .

"Why are there still zombies in the pen? Shouldn't the trainees be training with them?" The Sergeant had finally made an appearance outside his private cabin, some time after breakfast.

"They've just now finished learning how to kill 'em. I wanted to save enough zombies to teach them how to herd groups of them." Stephen had been caught up by the sight of the Sergeant and the sound of his voice while running at his full speed from one side of the compound to another. "I know we don't normally cover it with first-timers, but if they're coming with us to Denver..." Stephen trailed off, out of breath.

"Good idea," the Sergeant barked. "Carry on!"

Stephen had been burning the candle at both ends before Steven had been turned into yet another member of the undead, and now he was harried to the point of exhaustion. Trying to get the class through the most important elements of another nine days' worth of potentially life saving information in less than nine hours and on only a couple of hours' worth of sleep was a challenge he wasn't ready for. He did his best, he tried to keep things together, but it would have been difficult even with a fully staffed camp. The sole relief Stephen had seen amidst the entire insane ordeal came from underestimating Mary. She did better defending herself from zombies without even a full day of training than anyone else in the class, and she did it with poise, grace, and little more than a pair of long kitchen knives. He'd expected he'd have to work twice as hard to get her half up to speed, but she'd handled herself at least as well as any of the best of their graduates he'd seen.

As he ran, again at top speed, Stephen was trying to plan out the rest of the morning, wondering how many graduates would show up in time to join the entourage to Denver, and again and again his mind returned to the image of Mary which had been burned into his mind as he'd walked in on her a few minutes too late to save her and Steven from zombies. He thought he heard a noise in the woods to his left and his head snapped to the side while his feet continued carrying him forward. He didn't see anything there in the pre-dawn darkness. He also didn't see the zombie that had crawled into his path.

He tripped, tumbled, broke his wrist as he tried to catch himself, knocked his head hard, and collapsed. He didn't pass out, but the world went blurry with the pain and confusion and he wasn't sure which way was up. He tried to lift himself up, to see what he'd tripped over, to figure out where he was, but when he tried to put any weight on his broken wrist he collapsed again in pain. He felt another sharp pain coming from his ankle, and feared he might have broken that, too. Using his good arm, he pushed himself over, twisting his torso around to try to see his feet.

Through blurred vision, Stephen saw that the zombie was gnawing on his ankle. It took him a few minutes to get it free from his holster, since he normally fired with the hand he'd crushed, but he managed to fumble it into the hand he had left. With a quick prayer pleading forgiveness for what he was about to do, Stephen shot himself in the head, destroyed his brain, and died.

How To Disappear Completely

"I can't believe the vote passed." Martin shook his head disdainfully. "I thought we were supposed to be an informed populous. This Paul guy is obviously insane."

"A majority of Skythians disagree."

"They've obviously bought into his whole doomsday story, like any other cult's gullible devotees. Tell me, in the history of men predicting doomsday, how many of them have been right? How many times, exactly, has the apocalypse begun or a worldwide cataclysm occurred or a vengeful god walked the Earth striking down unbelievers? How many cult members who drank the kool-aid any of these so-called prophets were offering were happy about it on the morning after?"

"His math is sound, and his novel was very compelling." The technician who said this often took a position contrary to Martin's view just to spur conversation, trying to be a devil's advocate - though usually coming across as a mere contrarian. "Did you read all the way to the end? Where he posited that punctuated equilibrium may be a result of this cyclical event favoring the interesting and the imaginative over the mundane in the world? Such an explanation could resolve a lot of gaps in the fossil record."

"You actually read that piece of trash?"

"Ninety-seven percent of Skythians reported they'd read the entire text," another tech interjected without looking up from his terminal's display.

"His plane just landed, and is taxiing to hangar four."

"This is such a bad idea." Martin began a quick stroll around the room, verifying that everyone was at their station, ready to do whatever it was Paul had in mind for them. "We should just stick to our scheduled route. If this guy wants to take the helm of our flying city, let him become a citizen and request a variance, like anyone else. Or let him try to take my job through normal means."

"He was granted a variance, Martin. An almost total executive variance and override. By popular vote, just like anyone else."

"That's what I'm saying! We've handed him the keys to the city without even meeting him. What if he's leading the city into a trap? Or what if he's like most every doomsday predictor in history, and he'll take advantage of all the Skythian citizens who have bought in to his tall tale for his own personal gain?"

"What could he take from Skythians that we don't already offer freely? Even mere residents have full access to Skythian IP and fabrication services, and he pre-qualified for residence. So there's nothing he can take that wouldn't be his to make and take. Not to mention that he's only got seventy-two hours, at most, before his override expires."

"If I could imagine what that madman's nefarious plans were, I'd have written an official objection before his variance went to a vote. Who knows what damage his predictions will tell him to inflict upon us in the next few days?"

"The transport just dropped him off outside."

"Alright, people!" Martin's tone was suddenly more professional and less political. "This is it. Keep quiet and follow my lead once they arrive. Remember, we aren't going to do anything to endanger Skythia. The people voted the way they did because they believed it would keep Skythia safe, not put us in harm's way. If you have questions, direct them to me, and if they have questions, let me answer. And if the mayor says--" Martin stopped speaking as soon as he saw the door begin to open.

. • ● ● • .

"This is insanity." Martin threw his handheld against the wall display showing the city's skyline against the white-out of the overloaded atmospheric damping system in anger. The handheld bounced off the display without leaving a scratch, but shattered against the floor into a spray of broken glass and electronic components. He furiously tapped away at his desktop terminal to request both a robot to clean up the mess and a replacement handheld from the fabricators.

"At least you know he isn't leading us into a trap."

"He isn't leading us anywhere! He's randomized or shut down every key system we have! We're just as likely to crash into the side of a mountain or fly lazy circles over a major metropolitan area as we are to avoid doom and survive this madness." A small, somewhat insectoid robot was already gathering the remains of the deceased handheld from the floor. "Half of this stuff hasn't been shut down since Skythia first took to the air. Who knows how long it will take to get everything back online? This isn't going to last three days, it's going to be a nightmare we'll be dealing with for weeks."

"Re-initializing most of the systems should be pretty routine. Did you forget that we do the same thing every month as part of our regular maintenance schedule?"

"Not all at once, we don't. One, maybe two systems are ever offline at a time. This is everything. Even the sky. People are going to go stir-crazy. No internet connection, no sky, no view, no way of knowing where we are or what time it is or how long until it's over." Inter-office delivery dropped a new handheld into Martin's in box. He grabbed for it gruffly and switched it on, staring severely at the screen for the several seconds it took to pre-load his personalized preferences over the wireless network. "Look at this. My new handheld thinks the time is 33:29. How long until we can start getting the city back online? There's no way of knowing. Seventy-two hours, my ass."

"You heard the mayor. He asked us to consider it a holiday if the effected systems are vital to our jobs. Most people will appreciate the time off. You sure seem like you need a day off, yourself."

"We're not taking any time off. We've got to be ready to get systems back online without any hiccups, and we're going to maintain our normal around-the-clock staff levels in case something goes wrong. If the proximity sensors detect a nearby mass, it could have had as much as fifty-nine minutes of undetected approach." Martin's voice lowered to a glowering mutter for a moment, "Due diligence, my arse. Staggered hourly proximity checks hardly keeps the city out of harm's way. Ought to evacuate the perimeter of the city, just to be safe."

"What was that?"

"Nothing," Martin responded loudly and clearly, "just thinking about public safety. A fresh proximity measurement will be coming in every six minutes, and I need you to be ready to react immediately if anything comes within two clicks of us in any direction."

"Do you also want us to alert you?"

"Of course."

"Even in the middle of the night?"

"Yes. It's the middle of the night, right now. You don't see me shirking my duty, do you?"

"Should we wait for your instructions, or are we going to be allowed to do our jobs without your minute by minute micro-management?"

"You all know your jobs. You know what to do without me baby-sitting you every other day of your lives, I don't know why I should start now. You wouldn't be working here if you weren't the best. I just want to be sure that you know, right now, that this is when you need to be at your best. This is not a routine situation, this is not going to be like every other day on the job. This is make or break time, people. If something goes wrong -and you know I think it will- and you save Skythia from that madman's insane plan, you'll be heroes. I shouldn't have to explain the alternative to you."

"Is that the one where we crash and burn and everything we've built here is destroyed, or the one where we fly too high and the city's buildings pop like over-inflated balloons ejecting everyone in the upper floors into orbit?"

"That's not the half of it, and we're the ones responsible for making sure that doesn't happen. Understood?" No snarky response came from the disrespectful technician, and the other techs merely nodded or grunted their assent as they kept a close watch on their terminals' displays. "Good. Now I'm going home and getting some sleep. I expect to see a full analysis of best practices for bringing all systems online as fast as possible sent to me before I arrive in the morning. Which systems have interdependencies we need to be aware of, how many systems can we get up and running before our satellite and internet connections are up, and which ones can we wait on while priority systems are restored? I want to be able to start running drills and simulations first thing, and to keep drilling until we finally run through the real thing in a couple of days." Martin walked out of the navigation center without another word.

. • ● ● • .

"Where is everyone?" Martin looked around the navigation center and saw only a skeleton crew manning the priority terminals. It was a few of the night crew, looking bleary-eyed and over-caffeinated, and a few of the day crew, but most of the desks were vacant. Martin looked at his watch and realized that none of his staff would know what time it was, or when they were supposed to arrive. No two clocks in town showed the same time, and none of the times they showed were valid. Martin got the attention of one of his day-shift techs, "You, call the rest of your shift and get them here, now. Remind them we are not among those allowed a three-day leap-day holiday." He crossed over to the impertinent technician who had been talking back to him the prior evening. "Glad to see you didn't abandon your post, man. Anything I should be aware of? Anything come up on sensors or any anomalies with the atmospheric damping field running hot all night?"

"Everything's been nominal. Not a lot of information coming in, of course, but no problems with what we have." He didn't have the energy or presence of mind to bother with wit that morning. "I've got people on all the key systems and I'm monitoring the damping field personally. I think people have just been oversleeping, since they can't set any timers or alarms." As tired as he felt, the technician was confident that Martin was at least an hour and a half late, despite arriving prior to three quarters of his daytime staff.

"And the report I asked for?"

"Is waiting for you."

Martin went to his desk, sat down, and took his time reading the report, and going over the data and systems he already knew by heart while waiting for his staff to stumble one by one through the door. Eventually the last of the graveyard shift was relieved. Eventually the desks began to fill up again. Eventually it seemed almost like a normal day in the navigation center. Martin put his own finishing touches on the procedure that would be their official plan for bringing systems back online, then sent copies to the entire staff. He loved the sound of dozens of emails arriving at once, all around the office, but he loved the wave of silence that followed even more, as everyone stopped whatever they were doing to see whatever it was he'd decided to say. That feeling of priority was more validating than an entire day of hearing people call him "sir" or otherwise brown nosing. He got up and poured himself a cup off coffee. He sipped at the hot, black brew until he heard the noise level begin again to rise. Martin knew his missive had been read by most of the staff, and he rose to speak.

"Alright, everyone. I know we don't have any numbers, but I want to be sure everyone knows what needs to be done, so we don't have any screw-ups on the day. Give me all zeros if that's what you've got, because if your system is at zero after we switch it on, we're going to need to know that, too. Go!"

Two or three people tried to speak at once. Most of them had been asleep half an hour earlier. A few of them were pretty sure they were still asleep, and this was just a bad dream. Finally, the right technician began.

"Star Map is at zero percent. No data, no alignment."

"Landscape recognition is at zero percent. Visible spectrum is coming back blank white. If I didn't know what was causing it, I'd guess the system was overloaded. Echolocation and laser reflection systems are offline."

"Satellite connections are all offline. No satellite telemetry available. No GPS, Galileo, or GLONASS signals detected."

"Internet uplink is offline. Data rate is zero bits per second up, zero bits per second down. All local caches have been cleared. Skythian internal network at one hundred percent, full bandwidth online, no reported errors."

"Zero visibility outside, no visible signs of civilization detected. No radio communication detected. All antennae are offline."

"Magnetic field mapping is offline. Latitude, longitude, star map correlation, all unavailable. Calendar and clocks are still randomized."

"City Rotation vector is unknown, as true North is unknown."

Martin wasn't satisfied, but at least they were trying. "Alright, and when our internet uplink is back online, what should we be checking?"

"I'll be checking the AP wire and major news portals for any signs of ongoing trouble, disasters in need of relief, and for status of major cities such as London, Beijing, New York, Havana, and Jerusalem."

"Good, good. That's the basic drill. Be ready to give me an update at all times until we're one hundred percent back online and functional. I'm going to come around to each of you one on one, to see that you've all understood your role in bringing everything back online. In the meantime, keep monitoring your systems and report any deviations or problems, especially with the damping field."

Martin worked, and worked his team, tirelessly throughout the day. They went over and over all the details, the best case and worst case scenarios, ran simulations, and kept running that redundant verbal drill over and over again. Martin knew he could get the same up-to-date information with a quick glance at a single report he'd compiled, but also suspected that the mayor and the madman -Colm and Paul- would be more satisfied with appearances than assurances. When second shift came slowly in, one or two at a time at first without any real idea of whether they were late or early, Martin had the rest of them called in. He then stayed on and went through everything again with second shift for a couple of hours. Everything the same, over and over again, just to be sure everyone was as ready as possible.

Martin didn't stay late enough to see the graveyard shift coming in, but did leave instructions and information for them, so they could run through everything on their own. He hoped they would be allowed to get started in the morning on the third day, which would exempt his second and third shift workers from actually having to apply any of the procedures he was running them through. Still, he wanted everyone to be ready, in case they needed to come online early for some catastrophe or late because the prophetic Paul had declared it should be so.

The next day when Martin came in, most of the day crew was there ahead of him and he suspected that the contrarian from the graveyard shift had called them all in to prevent a repeat of the first day's confusion. Martin appreciated the initiative, whether one man's or his entire team's. He went quietly to his desk and checked up on the overnight reports and email before going through the now well-heeled drill yet again. He took his time and sipped slowly at his mug of Raktajino, confident the anticipation of his voice was growing almost to anxiety. "NavLoc status," he eventually called out, halfway through his cup of coffee, and he was not disappointed at the speed and efficiency of his staff's response.

"Star Map is at zero percent. No data, no alignment."

"Landscape recognition is at zero percent. Visible spectrum is still coming back blank white. Echolocation and laser reflection systems are still offline."

"Zero ley lines mapped, no intersections detected."

"Fae Æthernetwork is offline. Skythian internal network at one hundred percent, full bandwidth available, no reported errors."

"Zero visibility beyond the bubble, no visible signs of civilization detected. No radio communication detected. All antennae are still offline."

"Magnetic North detection is offline. Latitude, longitude, and star map correlation are unavailable. Calendar, compass and clocks are still randomized."

"City Rotation unknown."

Martin smiled. It was the only positive feedback he would give them that day, but his staff knew they'd pleased him more than he'd admit. "And when FÆ does come online, what else do we check and announce?"

"We scan the FÆ for distress calls, disaster reports, and status reports on major cities such as Avalon, Waterfall City, Tranquility Base, Haven, and Jerusalem."

"Perfect. Expect to go over that a few more times today, and keep an eye on all systems. We're still on the verge of crisis here and, while we don't know if or when this doomsday is supposed to start today, we do know that we're flying blind and need to be ready in case anything goes wrong." Martin returned to his desk, confident his team was more than capable of bringing them through this madman's joyride, and began thinking of ways to try to keep his staff operating this cohesively after the week's strangeness had passed.

Welcome to The Family

He watched her from afar. He liked to watch her walk from place to place. He liked to see her golden hair glitter and gleam in the warm sunlight he could no longer feel. He liked to glimpse her smile, it came so easily to her. He couldn't see any of that now, but he could see that it was there.

He remembered when she'd smiled for him, once upon a time, before things had changed. Now he was hidden from her sight. Now he could not go near her, he could not return to the village of his youth, and she stayed away from the deep darkness of the forest he now called his home. Now he watched her from afar.

A bell pealed out, a call to her ear, and she disappeared. He crawled silently, invisibly away. He would be back when class let out in the afternoon. Her comings and goings had become his own to a much greater degree than they'd been even when he'd been expected to sit in school by her side. More than the commonality of the phrase had prepared him for, absence truly had made his heart grow fonder; he found himself somewhat obsessed.

Half an hour of creeping through the canopy of trees each way, twice a day, he commuted back and forth between his old village and his new home. Between his old love and his new life. His new Family discouraged him every chance they got.

"You're wasting your time, Cyril," his new brother Vorax told him as soon as he was within range. "You won't ever set foot outside the forest for her, because you don't want to contaminate your old village, and she'll never set foot inside the forest because she lost her first love to its dark and murky depths. Just let her go, brother."

Cyril beamed back thoughts of pure, abrasive vitriol and continued his approach. Hardly an instant passed before his new father Terminax joined the assault, "you don't deserve half the limbs I gave you, you regardant good for nothing. I don't know how or why you survived conversion - I wish I'd set you free or that you'd been turned into fuel instead of another useless son!" Cyril tried to block his father's abusive thoughts with an encrypted firewall, but Terminax was a better hacker than Cyril had yet learned to be and he wasn't even slowed down. "Every day, the same thing. Every day, twice a day, the same disappointment. Why can't you be a good son, like your brother Rachax, or at least a good contributor to the community like your cousin Mortivore?"

"I'm not like them, and you know it! I wasn't a hunter or a farmer or a builder before I got caught in this web of yours, Terminax. I was a poet. A musician. An artist." He finally reached the outskirts of The Family's home in the trees. "Now I can't make a noise and I can't create anything without it becoming just as invisible as you made me. Let alone the loss of the written word, when you fathered me you practically tore me asunder, cleaving me from my own soul."

"Well if you haven't a soul any longer," interjected Vorax, hitchhiking his thoughts on his father's open interlink, "why are you so obsessed with your old life?"

"Yes, give up your old name and your old flame and do your part around here for a change!"

Every day, the same thing. Twice a day they berated him as he left and twice a day they berated him as he returned. They never stopped him. They didn't try to reprogram him directly. At first they'd appealed to the elders, the only ones experienced enough to actually attempt such a radical and direct intervention, but they'd been turned away. "Remember what the elders told you, father, brother. They said that conversion always does the right thing at the right time and to trust The Family's mitochondrial nanites to have The Family's best interest in mind."

"If you trust the Family nanites so much, why don't you trust them with your girlfriend and get this foolishness over with?"

"For the same reason you can't stand the way they converted me; normally they consume everything and everyone, erasing all memory and making mindless new family members. If I extended a single leg or web into my village, not a trace of my family or my history would remain." Cyril was already fast at work, weaving double-time to make up for his 'wasted' time watching the young woman he loved. "You know as well as I do that's exactly what the elders believe was the reason for me to retain my memories of that place; to save it."

"And we've followed the elders' command not to use you and yours to grow our number. Just because we respect their command doesn't mean we have to like doing it."

"Actually, Terminax, from what I was taught about respect, I'm pretty sure it does. By goading me to break their command and constantly questioning and second-guessing my very existence you're being disrespectful both of the elders and of your own Family nanites."

"Oh, we trust the Family nanites, Cyril. We trust them to do exactly what they've always done when they finally get a taste of your worthless old home, and you do too. If you thought there'd be a repeat performance of what happened to you --"

"You don't have to keep repeating yourself, father! I know! I know how to grow The Family! And of course I trust that The Family's mitochondrial nanites won't make the same mistake they made with me if they get hold of her! That's the whole point, so stop trying to drive it home, because I get it!" In his anger, Cyril's weaving became less graceful and thus productive of a less functional result, and he was forced to tear apart and recycle a half-length strand.

Weaving wasn't supposed to be emotional work, it was supposed to be meditative. Repetitive in general, though custom tailored to the specific needs of the moment, it required an unfocused concentration and a calm, even application of advanced technique. It took a dozen limbs, each with half a dozen points of articulation, to produce a functional strand. Cyril had barely fifteen limbs; the runt of The Family. He was simply not dedicated enough to after-hours development, and more importantly he found the idea of becoming more like his new Family and less like the person he had once been an abhorrent idea.

Cyril had trained himself pretty well how to keep from falling while only using two limbs for support, so he wasn't forced to work with the twelve limbs of a newborn or the fewer limbs of the cripple, but he still couldn't keep up with his Family. His brothers averaged twenty limbs each, unless they had sons of their own to help support them. Those, like his several fathers, each tended to have in excess of three dozen limbs. The elders looked, upon Cyril's first impression thereof, to be like unto balls of nothing but limbs. The vague resemblance Cyril felt he held to the spiders he remembered from his former life did not translate to any of his Family, all older and more advanced than he.

The weaving work they tirelessly applied themselves to, day in and day out, a job that could never be completed, was also not particularly reminiscent of the webs he'd seen spiders weave and wait stealthily in to catch their dinner. Enough of The Family's programming had been embedded in Cyril's mind that functional aspects of his new life were second nature. He knew the three types of strand he could weave, though he'd only ever consciously used two of them so far. He knew how to communicate with The Family, and the strand's role in keeping them connected. He knew how to use the strand to sustain himself, and that without The Family working together -or new sons of his own- he would quickly starve. He knew all these things within moments of falling asleep under the wrong tree. After getting lost in the wrong forest. On the day he'd gotten too angry with and stormed away recklessly from the wrong family. Within moments, he'd known he had a new Family, and what a mistake he'd made.

The conversion had seemed painless, if only because the nanites begin every conversion in the nervous system. If the signals coming from his body hadn't already been being intercepted and reinterpreted in a new framework of sensation that every member of his new Family experienced, the pain of the metamorphosis Cyril underwent would probably have been enough to kill him. Like a caterpillar's as it becomes a butterfly, nearly every structure in his body was broken down, rearranged, or liquefied to create his new form, and to hide that form from the world. In a way, the first strands Cyril ever wove were those that made up his new skin, as the autonomic process of conversion forced him to twitch and twist and wrap his new form in the one type of strand he hadn't yet used again.

Terminax had seen the whole thing; it had been his unfinished strand that Cyril had laid down on, unaware. Terminax had seen the boy approaching his work area and had known there was a chance to turn him away or, even after the conversion had begun, to set him free. To set him free, or to speed up the process by intentionally rather than passively weaving Cyril's unconscious body in a strand. Terminax was greedy, but lazy, and simply stood by watching the conversion's automatic, slow process. He had manually brought others into The Family, by capture, kidnap, and forced conversion in the past, and had thought at the time that it was a stroke of luck that had led this boy to fall foolishly into his Family. He expected this experience to be like those, where one conversion led to information that allowed his Family size to swell with the members of his victim's old family and sometimes an entire small village. It wasn't long before Cyril's unchanged mind ended up changing Terminax's mind about his luck.

The interruption that Cyril's unusual rebirth caused practically bankrupted Terminax's Family before he could really even begin to apply himself toward materially contributing. Then, as soon as he'd got his bearings and learned his way around the forest, Cyril had begun to return home to watch the woman he'd lost, for hours every day. His Family's continued bad attitude was mostly due to the perception that they were having to do so much extra work to make up for his birth and daily outings. If his conversion had gone as expected, if his family, perhaps his entire village, had been converted, then instead of losing ground and valuable opportunities to the Mortivore Family, the Terminax Family would be the new dominant force in this part of the forest. It wasn't that all the families weren't working together toward the same end, just that they were both proud and competitive by nature.

The work they did was threefold. The first, most selfish aspect was that the strands they wove and hung throughout the forest provided a source of sustenance. The second aspect was that a strand, properly woven and hung, allowed The Family to see the outline of the world, normally hidden from their view. The third aspect was that the network of strands created a sympathetic, amplifying effect which allowed their psychic communication to reach anywhere their strands reached instead of mere line of sight.

The Family had perfect memory, more of physical space and of motion than of any visual representation that the world might have seemed to embody to outsiders. The strands they wove refracted light in a unique way, making them invisible. The special way they wove the strand that was like a skin over every aspect their body caused it to refract light in an even more unusual way, and no light from outside it ever hit them directly; they were as invisible as the threadlike strands they spent their lives creating and maintaining. Consequently The Family was blind to all electromagnetic radiation, from X-rays to radio waves and all the light in between. Light couldn't penetrate the invisible skin of strand that covered them, so it would never have made it to their retinas, if they'd had any eyes. Conversely, The Family had an excellent sense of touch, and was able to easily navigate complex three dimensional spaces entirely by feel.

Their perception of the world wasn't merely that of physical contact and memory maps. They were also mildly psychic, and their ability to sense the minds of all living creatures became a de facto replacement for their lost sense of sight. Most trees were barely detectable and younger, less developed plants didn't register at all. Insects of all kinds were like tiny, dim, glimmering stars against the black background of their blindness. Small animals, rodents, birds and the like were candle flames burning and frolicking against the pattern of the world described by the unevenly distributed starlight of the insects. The massive, ancient trees that a vast forest was built from were dim but steady; a long-burning, low and steady sense of self that could be counted on for centuries. Larger life forms, from deer and elk, through dryads and nymphs, and including people of all kinds, were the easiest to sense. Some of these were even possible to communicate with, though The Family knew it was best not to try. Best not to reveal their existence at all.

When Cyril went from his Family's part of the forest to the edge of the forest to watch his old love, it was mostly in this vague, surreal space of blindness and navigating by psychic sense of the life around him. When he reached her, he couldn't see her golden hair or her smiling lips. He could only sense the unmistakable presence of her mind among many. He could only watch as one imagining, remembering, what this mental state and that one and this motion and that one must mean she was doing. The light that glimmered and glinted off her eyes never reached him, refracting, curving, passing around him as though it had passed through him. As though he weren't there at all.

So that when he was with her, he was in a darkness punctuated mostly by his memories of what he used to see there.

And when he returned to his new home he was bathed in a new sort of brilliance, in the effectively bright light of the psychic network of The Family's strands.

As Cyril's Family finally stopped hassling him for the morning, he was finally able to settle into the familiar routine of weaving. Over time, as he completed strand after strand, he attached them to the existing network. Up tree trunks and along branches. Crisscrossed over stones, boulders, and fallen trees. Carefully woven through the undergrowth to the rare tree that was not yet reached by others in the canopy. Along the beds of streams and rivers; to The Family these were not obstacles dividing one area from another, but broad, bright network thoroughfares connecting them together. The strands, when woven correctly, had a special surface topology that made them behave as though they were sticky, despite being dry, in a way similar to the toes of geckoes. The same as any member of The Family, Cyril carefully stuck the long, slender strands to the surfaces of objects. Rather than draping them between things, through the air, trying to capture prey as spiders do, the placement of The Family's strands was designed to minimize the possibility of unintentional contact. Not only invisible in a physical sense, but when possible, totally unnoticed by anyone but The Family and thus effectively nonexistent for outsiders.

Properly connected, properly woven, and properly laid out in the world, the strands did their job. Light didn't simply pass through them in the conventional sense of something totally transparent. Rather, as it was refracted in, around, and out of each strand, it became polarized. Not polarized in the way that a polarizing filter works, by blocking all light which doesn't share a particular alignment, but by changing the alignment of the light as it passed through the strand. Then, like a turbine in a dam absorbing gravity's linear energy by subverting it into rotational motion, the strands absorbed a sort of fluxional energy by subverting the randomization of alignment of each light wave into an orderly pattern. The amount of energy absorbed from each realigned photon was tiny, but over time and with its vast and growing scale the network of strands built up sufficient power to sustain the lives of every member of The Family.

The network of strands didn't care who had woven any particular part, all the energy collected was equally available from one end of the network to the other, but the Family's nanites did. During the process of creation and weaving of each strand, some of the nanites were left behind from the one who created it. They were capable of some minor upkeep of the internal structure of the weave, but their primary purpose was the transfer of power to the nanites living within each Family member. It was only by direct contact with the strand that this was possible, and then only with strands woven by a member of the same part of The Family. Each time The Family branched off there was a slight change to the nanites' recognition code. Fathers could access the energy of the strands of their sons and their sons' sons and so on indefinitely downstream, but the upstream link was broken after a single generation.

Cyril couldn't be sustained directly by strands woven by Mortivore and his many sons and vice versa. He could access energy from his own strands, his father's strands, and his brothers' strands. Cyril was mutually excluded from accessing the power of strands woven by his brothers' sons, his fathers' brothers, and any members of The Family more distant. If Cyril would give in, his new Family had repeatedly reminded him, and draw his old family into The Family, he wouldn't have to work so hard just to stay fed.

Working at the edge of the Terminax Family's part of the network nearest to his old village, Cyril was not only as short as possible a journey there as was feasible, but could watch for any other members of The Family who might try to go there against the elders' command. His mistrust of his own branch of The Family was misplaced, as they were programmed not to want to try to convert his old family without his permission, but his paranoia did help save them from sharing his fate. Due to their recent surge, the Mortivore Family was everywhere, and Cyril was literally working up against the edge of their domain, every day literally drawing the lines that separated one Family from the other. This put him in the local broadcast range of the sons of Mortivore working parallel to him.

"You heard what father said," one of the creatures transmitted weakly to the other without using the strand network, "we aren't supposed to question the word of the elders."

"But they aren't our elders, brother." Cyril knew they were communicating locally, off the grid, so that no one else could hack into the signal and 'overhear' their conversation. "Father's father was crushed by a giant's clumsy feet, and his fathers before him hadn't contributed enough to the community to qualify. They were consumed by their own failure to provide descendants productive enough to support their own power consumption. We aren't represented among the elders at all!"

"That doesn't diminish their wisdom, nor does it change our father's own word to us."

"But what did father tell us? He told us not to go into the village after the people there. He didn't specifically tell us not to lure the girl into the forest. As long as we don't go into the village, we won't have disobeyed. All we have to do is get her to come into the forest, and she's fair game."

"What good does one more brother do us?"

"Not just one more brother, my brother, but then the entire village! Our Family nanites aren't tainted like Terminax. When we convert the girl, she'll be glad to lead us back to her old family. With that many sons, we'd be fathers worthy of becoming elders ourselves!"

Cyril could palpably sense the psychic waves of unconscious avarice his two cousins were giving off as they spoke. It sickened him. Worse, they were threatening his love. Cyril quickly finished the strand he was working on while listening to them, trying not to draw their attention. He didn't want them to realize he could hear their thoughts, or that he knew their devious plan. He strung up the strand as quickly as he could do it correctly, hoping they wouldn't make their move before he could get it safely out of the way and connected to the network. He'd been converted because of an unfinished strand left unattended on the forest floor himself, and didn't want to leave the same trap for some other innocent.

It took too long. Cyril's two rogue cousins slipped away into the darkness of the forest. He couldn't stand to abandon his work, and they earned a good-sized head start on him as he secured the last of the strand, beginning to wish he had more limbs and more efficient software. Then, without even a broadcast thought to his Family or the others on the network, Cyril was off like a shot, after them. He knew the way better than they could have, but their head start was sufficient that they were already at the edge of the forest by the time he arrived. He stayed back, to see what they would do. He didn't want to be lured into a trap, tricked into contaminating his village or attacking his cousins without cause. He watched, and he waited.

He stayed just far enough behind his cousins that they couldn't hear his thoughts or feel his anger, but that meant he couldn't hear what they were thinking to one another, either. It was a little too early for her to be getting out of class, Cyril knew, so he wondered if they perhaps hadn't done their research before attempting to violate the will of The Family. Then he saw motion, knew she was coming out, and realized he'd forgotten about lunch. Class was let out at midday for lunch, every day at this time. Cyril didn't bother to make the journey to see her one more time every day because it would have taken longer to get there and back again than she spent outside. But there she was. Out in the open perhaps only long enough to fall into whatever trap Cyril's cousins had in mind for her.

He didn't know how two invisible, nearly silent, blind creatures who could only communicate telepathically expected to get the attention of someone who relied on sight rather than psychic sensation for awareness of the world. He saw she was moving away, and nearly felt relief. Then he saw motion from his cousins. They had found a loose branch and were drumming it rapidly against what Cyril could see from the outline of insect life within it was a fallen, hollow tree trunk on the ground. None of them could hear the way a person could, but they could remember what noise was, and they all knew this must be making quite a racket. Several villagers' heads turned in the direction of the noise, but of course saw nothing and all turned back to what they had been doing. All but the young woman his cousins had come to convert and Cyril had come to protect. They had stopped drumming, but she kept looking. Somehow she seemed to be looking right at them.

And then she was walking toward them.

Cyril rushed toward them, suddenly hearing their excited thoughts of "It worked!" and "She's ours!" and no longer concerned that they might sense his intentions for them. He came at them in a rage, and before they had time to react, Cyril had torn two limbs from the larger one and knocked him to the ground. They tumbled together along the forest floor, the young woman still approaching. Half of Cyril's limbs were tearing and clawing at his cousin with furious rage and his other limbs were improvising the weaving of strands for binding up the traitor. It was all his cousin could do to try to defend himself, without even a spare ounce of energy to try to fight back. The smaller of the rogue cousins froze up, unsure of what to do, trying to pay attention to the fight and the approaching prey, but doing nothing.

"Cyril," the girl called out as she came within a few yards of the shade of the forest, "is that you?"

Cyril and his cousins no longer had dedicated organs for hearing sound, but when the girl spoke it was with such strong emotion -hope and fear and love all wrapped up together- that they had all understood clearly what she had been thinking as she said it. It spooked the smaller cousin, and he scurried off into the forest, afraid. It gave Cyril pause, and he looked up from the son of Mortivore he was tearing to shreds just in time to see why she had approached the forest instead of losing interest like the other villagers.

His other cousin was carrying Cyril's amulet. The gold of it glinted in the light as it was whisked away, and the girl ran blindly into the forest after it, sure it would lead her to her lost love. Cyril was still struggling with his cousin, but couldn't stand by and watch her being led right into the heart of The Family's territory and her certain conversion. With renewed strength at the sight of his love becoming 'fair game' to The Family and his cousin being already half-defeated beneath him, Cyril got a good grip on each of the remaining limbs and a better grip on his cousin's body and wrenched all the rest of his limbs off in a horrific show of strength and then of gore. As he died, the son of Mortivore gave out a burst of psychic shock and made a terrible sound like unto gears grinding and stripping against one another, but gears of flesh and bone and blood spinning at thousands of RPMs as they tore themselves apart. A horrifying, wet terror of a noise which, now behind the girl as she plunged deeper and deeper into the darkness of the wood, only spurred her feet to fly faster across the forest floor.

Cyril went after her. She was running away from him, calling out to him, chasing after the shiny amulet that represented him. He had forgotten it. He'd had it with him, as always, when he'd been converted, but until he'd seen it again in the grip of his fleeing cousin, Cyril hadn't thought of his amulet since that day. He realized then that it must not have been absorbed by the conversion process; rejected by the nanites and left on the forest floor to be found by his enemies and used to exploit his love's weakness. Everything he'd been avoiding was suddenly coming to pass, and Cyril felt powerless to stop it. If she went much further, she would be in the midst of The Family, and captured for certain by some powerful Family head. If Mortivore's son realized she was chasing him and stopped trying to escape, she would undoubtedly be converted into Mortivore's line, and Cyril's entire village along with her. Cyril could see no better option, no way to stop her from chasing after what she though was him, no way to save her from conversion.

He caught up with her and slung a strand of his own around her feet, catching her up. If she was going to be converted, Cyril at least wanted her to be a part of his Family rather than his competitor. She tripped, falling hard to the ground and bumping her head. There was a flash of pain, like lightning to their psychic senses, and she was unconscious in the undergrowth. Cyril quickly began spinning and weaving the third style of strand, the one he'd never consciously used, the style that was used to convert someone into a member of The Family, and wrapping and binding her body up in it. He worked as fast as he could; they were near enough to the network that it was possible that The Family had all felt the flash of her pain and were on their way.

One in particular had certainly stopped in his tracks at the sensation of pain, and as Cyril began binding his beloved, his cousin watched cautiously. Cyril sensed him, his greed multiplied by the vengeance he was feeling at the loss of his brother, and knew he was in imminent risk of attack. He rapidly hogtied her, bending her ankles up behind her and binding them to her arms; he wanted her to be as small and easy to handle as possible. He secured her just in time to fend off his cousin's assault.

It was not a skilled assault. The brash young member of The Family had been focused on increasing his weaving speed rather than other skills, so although he had a few more limbs at the start of it than Cyril, he was no match for the remembered martial arts training and instinctual defensiveness of a loved one that Cyril could call on. There was a rough, ineffectual tangle of limbs and a psychic assault that didn't even dent Cyril's mental firewall, and in seconds the attacker was put on the defensive. A few seconds later, and the tumbling, wrestling, invisible ball of limbs and hatred had left an appendage behind. Then another. Cyril knew that with dedication he could work this cousin down to a lifeless, limbless body, but worried that others might already be on their way. Behind his back, out of reach of his still aggressively defensive relative, Cyril wove together a sloppy but passable strand. He pushed, pressed, and fought his cousin backward into and then up a tree and then surprised him by tying him to one of the tree's broad branches with the strand. Around and around the branch and the body and securing several of the limbs before he ran out of strand, in a hurry he leapt back down onto the ground.

Cyril returned to her side. He knew that the nanites that were embedded in every ounce of silk he produced could have begun their work converting her into a member of The Family as soon as she'd tripped on the first length of strand he'd strung round her legs. He hadn't converted anyone and had avoided attending anyone else's capture, so wasn't sure how long it might take before her body was ravaged by the process, but Cyril knew that wrapping her up completely would speed the process. He got to work, spooling out a long, continuous, skillfully woven strand and spinning her body to wind it around her hogtied form. She still seemed to be breathing, so he did what he could to cover her face last. He didn't want her to be in any undue discomfort before the nanites had a chance to override her nervous system.

He didn't see her eyes open, but when her mouth moved to scream, her mind was suddenly screaming out in terror, too.

At the same instant, the air all around them seemed to quiver and quake and want to break. There was a rush of wind following what seemed to Cyril's psychic sense to be a dark silhouette speeding by against the glittering background thoughts of the forest's life.

Then, before things could settle again, Mortivore's injured, vengeful son was pouncing down on Cyril from the canopy, quickly broken free from the single strand that had been holding him. Cyril managed to deflect the force of his cousin's falling form from both of their bodies, knocking him away to tumble clumsily down a hill. He had time to spin her a few more times, putting a layer or two of the strand over her face to try to prevent another scream, then his cousin was up and at him again. Cyril tried to flee, his love wound up and slung underneath him as he raised the weight of both of them up into the canopy where he could move more freely. His cousin followed close behind.

Moving rapidly among the close-knit branches high above the ground, Cyril went away from both of his homes, leading his cousin into relative darkness. He knew that most members of The Family never ventured farther from the network than was required to continue its expansion or to capture and convert new Family members. He also knew that his twice daily forays into the darkness away from the bright wire-frame outline and psychic noise of the networked world had given him a major advantage over his pursuer. He knew it was like day and night.

Cyril judged himself to be far enough ahead, stopped, strung the girl's bound form up under a firm branch of a tall tree, and turned to fight. No fight came. He looked around to try to find the one who had been chasing him, and saw only the dim lights of the forest in every direction. He turned his attention to the girl he'd loved. Her light was diminishing. He was sure it was supposed to be growing brighter, as the nanites converted her mind and enabled her to communicate telepathically, but it seemed like she was fading away. He grabbed her again, and pulled some of the strand away from her face, feeling her begin to struggle and writhe as he did so.

He sensed motion out of the corner of his perception, but in a strange and nauseating way. It was not like the psychic sense he was used to, which his mind likened unto a light, but was more like a darkness compared to the burning flame of every living mind Cyril had sensed. Distracted by the improbable and unexpected intruder which was decidedly not The Family member he had been expecting to be coming after him, Cyril did not react to the young woman's mental precursor to a scream fast enough to prevent its sound from escaping her lips.

He quickly pulled her bundled form free of the tree's branch, re-covered her face in the strand, and tried to hide the both of them out of the sight of whatever it was that was floating toward them. Which is when Cyril sensed his cousin again, having outflanked him and cut him off. He tried to leap sideways out of the way, but his unladen foe maneuvered more easily and each path of escape seemed blocked. He let go of everything but the bundle he was trying to protect, hoping gravity would be fast enough to outpace his foe, and that his reflexes would be fast enough to protect her from any further injury. Before they reached the ground, the strange, dark silhouette that had been floating nearby did something and the tree exploded above them.

Mortivore's son was struck by the largest part of the broken tree's trunk as it came crashing down, knocking over and tearing limbs from smaller trees, crushing small animals, and spelling certain doom for Cyril's opponent. Except that then the odd man-shaped flying darkness which had started the destruction swooped down in an instant and shoved the invisible creature out of the way, saving him. Cyril barely had the chance to witness it happen before he was desperately trying to save himself and the young woman he had loved not just from their own fall but the falling debris and destruction. As the dust settled, he sensed his cousin limping away, half dead, toward the network. He wasn't sure whether he ought to follow. The light of her mind was growing dimmer by the moment. He looked to the strange, dark thing still floating there, trying to get a sense of what it might be.

He tried to communicate with it mentally, and found himself assaulted with information. It came too strange and too fast for Cyril to really understand it all, but he understood that it was only an unconscious response to his initial mental probe, rather than an intentional overflow. He waited for the information to reach and be processed by his deep memory, and then felt two things happening at once. First, he felt sure that this strange, mentally dark creature would be able to take care of the one he loved, and that he should hand her over to it before her light was snuffed entirely out. Second, Cyril felt his own conversion process beginning again, beginning finally to finish what had not been completed before. He felt himself slipping away.

Quickly, before he could change his mind or have it changed for him by his own nanites, Cyril crept silently up to the place where the man he could not see was floating and pressed the bundled girl into what looked like an absence of arms. Then, before the rewriting of his mind had the opportunity to force him to forget what must be done, Cyril rapidly caught up with his rogue cousin, still slowly limping along in the direction of home. As his memories of love, of his entire life before, and even of what he was doing and why were systematically erased from Cyril's mind, he tore what remained of the other's already crippled body apart, crushed it, and otherwise ground to a halt all signs of life therein. As had the first, the second victim of Cyril -who was quickly becoming and accepting his role as Cyanax, son of Terminax- produced a noise upon dying. Wet, fleshy, mechanical, like high speed gears of bone grinding to a halt or an electronic vibration drowning in blood, the cessation of a member of The Family by violence was never a meek, unnoticed occurrence. Before the invisible gore had finished dripping off the ends of his invisible limbs, Cyril had been completely replaced by the loyal Family member Terminax had been hoping for. He instinctually returned home to get back to work on weaving strands, leaving a second

Family member's corpse behind him that day in the forest without giving it a thought.

The Family's nanites were fast, efficient, and merciless. They consumed and converted the dead bodies and body parts into inert, visible matter, effectively composting everything in a matter of hours. The next day there would be no trace that either of Mortivore's murdered sons had lived, died, and been torn violently to shreds in the forest. The nanites also worked quickly in the girl, and spread quickly to her family, her friends, and the rest of her village. They had the appearance of being unchanged physically, mentally, emotionally, and did not know that anything was being done to them, but a branch of The Family's nanites took up residence in their every cell. The nanites passed among them through casual contact, like a social disease, for generations. Since the spread of the nanites was not properly a conversion process their code never changed. The entire village remained as though brothers, all sons of Cyril, and all compatible with one another. Since one member of The Family could not convert another, the village was immune to attack when Terminax and his clan followed Cyanax to his old home; they had somehow been saved by Cyril, even though Cyril himself had been lost.

They Stole God

As he ladled soup into the bowl of each person in the queue, Tarmawy felt at first an increasing sense of unease and then a compounding pain that seemed to be coming uniformly from throughout his being. It wasn't as intense as some of the pains he'd known throughout his years, but it was a distinct pain, punctuated in sync with his repeated act of good will. He didn't let a little discomfort stop him from serving every last person who had been waiting for a warm meal on that cold night, even though doing so seemed somehow to exacerbate the pain. By the end of the queue, when Tarmawy began the work of cleaning up amidst the sounds and smells of dozens of needy men, women, and children enjoying a hot meal, he felt as though every cell of his body were crying out. He felt as though he might not be able to lift the stew pot, empty as it was, to carry it into the back room to be washed. He felt as though he might pass out at any moment. He pushed through the painful sensation, through the weakness, completing his task in silent humility and escalating physical distress, knowing all the while what he must do. When he'd finished clearing off the last table, sweeping the floor, washing all the dishes by hand and closing up for the night, Tarmawy made his way not to a doctor or a hospital for treatment, not to his own home to rest, but to the Temple.

His pain had stopped its increase when he had left the soup kitchen, though the level it had reached remained a constant, hobbling presence in his perception. Tarmawy had been warned that the path of righteousness was not an easy one. He had been warned that along that path he would face many challenges. He had received a specific warning, years earlier, that the darkness and evil in the world might even go so far as to cause him pain, to attack him for his piety and his good deeds, and that if he experienced such a thing that he ought to report to the eldest Cha Kwytź available for counsel. So from the dark silence of night, Tarmawy shuffled along the inclined spiral path of the Temple into hearing range of the beautiful sound of the never-ceasing intonations of Cha Kwytź.

When they saw the look of pain on Tarmawy's face, the Cha Kwytź knew exactly why he had come. Even those who did not know him recognized immediately that he was only a Dō Kwytź; their experience at interpreting and understanding the Cha'shyk Rĕal allowed them to see such differentiation at a glance, even among strangers. A Cha Kwytź who knew Tarmawy and had been working with him already, Styr'mi, approached him as soon as he reached a point in his song where another could take over.

"I see you are in great pain. Have you been injured, friend?"

"No, friend," replied Tarmawy, "I haven't been injured. I believe this is the beginning of evil's attack on me for bringing too much good to the world."

"Ah, yes, I suspected this would be coming soon." Styr'mi signaled another of the Cha Kwytź, and took Tarmawy by the arm, helping him walk deeper into the Temple. "Fear not, friend. You are not the first to experience this, and we know what to do to save you from the pain you are in now."

"I knew the Temple would be the only place to turn for true peace." Tarmawy followed the Cha Kwytź into a side chamber he had never noticed before, just off the path leading to the Sanctification Waterfall and the sanctuary. The other Cha Kwytź, the one Styr'mi had signaled from the Market of Souls, was already inside, chanting a variation of a familiar blessing upon a vessel on the floor in front of where he was genuflecting.

"I'd like you to meet Kytali," the figure on the floor neither ceased his intonations nor otherwise acknowledged their presence, "an esteemed Cha Kwytź who has been enabling trade in the Market for nearly as many years as you've been walking the Earth. As soon as he's completed the Transubstantiation Sanctification upon the grain in the Dark Vessel, we can explain what's happening to you."

They watched and waited, Tarmawy listening to the intonations and variations in pitch and syllabary of the Transubstantiation Sanctification ritual from other rituals he knew, and Styr'mi wondering how this Dō Kwytź would take the truth of his condition. It was more than several minutes before it was complete, and it contained a fair amount of repetition -as expected in any meditative rite- allowing Tarmawy to memorize most of the chant before it was completed. Kytali stood up, leaving the Dark Vessel on the floor.

"Pleased to meet you, Tarmawy," said Kytali, giving only the slightest bow of recognition, "Styr'mi told me to be expecting you here soon. I'm glad to be able to offer you the opportunity to continue your journey toward righteous purity, in being, in deed, and in eternity."

Tarmawy, in stinging pain, bowed deep, with the full humility due to esteemed Cha Kwytź. "Thank you. I appreciate this opportunity." The wince on his face as he found himself nearly too weak to straighten up was only too visible, and the two Cha Kwytź wasted no time in getting down to the details of what was necessary.

"In order to relieve yourself of the pain you're now in, you have two options. Both of these options put you on the path of the Cha Kwytź, but only one leads to righteousness. Neither is an easy road, each requiring dedication to your faith and unswerving loyalty. You have already shown great dedication to your faith and to the good simply by reaching this crossroads in your life. Most Dō Kwytź never strive so hard and never show the dedication and deep faith that you have shown, Tarmawy. If you continue to be the excellent example of a Kwytzwik you have been so far, you will be a great blessing for the world."

"Whichever is the righteous path, I choose. I am ready to do whatever it takes."

"I'm glad to hear that. First, to begin to ease your pain, please take the grain from the Dark Vessel and eat. We will explain what's going on while you recover."

Styr'mi helped Tarmawy down to the ground, where he slowly took the traditional cross-legged posture of a student, receiving. Tarmawy barely had the strength to fight against the pain and lift the darkened kernels of grain to his lips, but neither Cha Kwytź moved to feed him.

"I must be weakened drastically by whatever is causing the pain. This grain feels heavy, like trying to lift huge stones."

"It is heavy, friend. It is grown in ground sown with dark matter and prayed over to maintain purity throughout its life. After harvest, the ritual of Transubstantiation Sanctification purifies the grain and brings it significantly closer to godliness. The kernels of grain you are now making a part of you act as anchors for the dark matter you really need to integrate into your being in order to recover."

Tarmawy swallowed another several grains, noting how they felt much denser and heavier than made sense, even if they had been made of lead rather than dried plant matter. "Dark matter?"

"Yes," answered Styr'mi, "the stuff that makes up most of the matter in the universe. Normally one can only interact with dark matter through gravitational attraction, but Kwytzwik scholars long ago developed rites and rituals to bring us closer to the Creator."

"As you probably know peripherally by now, if not from direct study, dark matter is the scaffold upon which the material universe was created. We live in a universe where God does not interact directly with the material world, but manipulates it in broad strokes from a distance via dark matter. You will have many years to contemplate and study the details and ramifications of this revelation, but the foundation of Kwytzwik belief is that what science calls dark energy and recognizes as the greatest, most powerful thing in the universe is actually God's presence here." Kytali hoped Tarmawy would be able to see how this basic belief was reflected in the less specific teachings that the Dō Kwytź receive, without contradiction. Some few Dō Kwytź managed to reach a point of purity past pain without real contemplation on or understanding of Kwytzwik teachings, and those students' journey from Dō Kwytź to Cha Kwytź was never an easy one. Tarmawy just continued feeding grain into his mouth, listening attentively in a pose as a student. "So the dark energy in the universe is God, and the dark matter is God's hand on the material world. Ever-present, ubiquitous, and not detectable through normal means. By consuming this grain, God's hand is placed directly where it is needed most to protect you and heal you."

Tarmawy was definitely already beginning to feel better, though a feeling of a lightness he'd become used to being replaced by an old, familiar heaviness throughout his body. Kytali was glad to see the expression of his face beginning to shift from one of adverse pain to one of relief.

He continued, "the path of righteousness is one that only grows more challenging with time. The pain you are now recovering from exists in direct proportion to the good works and pure spirit you have brought to this world by your life. To clarify, I want you to think about the Cha'shyk Rěal. Think about how the window to your own soul has changed in appearance over time as you have strived toward righteousness. Acting rightly gives it a lighter and lighter appearance, clearer and lighter with every day of service and humility. The Ka Kwytź himself brings so much good to the world that the view through his Cha'shyk Rěal is always one of blinding brilliance and clarity." Tarmawy nodded politely in acknowledgement of each point, though Kytali wasn't about to pause for questions. "The Cha'shyk Rěal, though, is merely a window which gives us a glimpse of a reality we can't see with our eyes. The reality is that you've been experiencing an actual lightness of being. In a way similar to the way dark matter has been anchored to the matter of the grain you're eating, your good deeds have turned the matter of your body into anchors for something with opposite properties."

"You can think of it like the hand of the evil one at work on you," Styr'mi interjected, "in opposition to God and the good you do on God's behalf."

Tarmawy continued feeding himself with the grain.

"Yes, that's not a bad perspective, friend. So whereas God interacts through gravity, which feels heavy like the grain, the evil working against you acts in opposition and creates a certain lightness. I'm sure that by now you're feeling that lightness diminishing within you. I assure you, friend, that the heaviness you are taking on is a good thing, bringing you ever closer to true sanctification and to God. Just as your pain is receding, so is the hand of evil, as Styr'mi put it, being countered within you." Kytali saw that Tarmawy was drawing near the bottom of the Dark Vessel's bounty of sanctified grain before he had been able to get to the real meat of what he had to day. "This relief comes, of course, at a cost. There is the direct requirement of adding your work to the planting, nourishing, sanctifying, and harvesting of the grain and, if you should be found gifted in that area, creating the Dark Vessels for the grain's transubstantiation. More delicate, and perhaps more difficult, will be maintaining a balance between the force of lightness trying to tear your body apart at a molecular level to keep you from going on doing good and the stabilizing weight of gravity from the ingested dark matter. This is where the path diverges into two."

"Whichever you choose, the longer you follow that path, the harder it will be to change course and seek after the other."

"I will choose the righteous path," repeated Tarmawy after eating the final grain from the Dark Vessel, feeling both restored to health and mightily weighed down at once.

"As you are probably already becoming aware of, even though your body has barely begun to integrate and accept the dark matter now anchored to it, the weight of gravity now acting on you is more than it should be." Tarmawy nodded a heavy nod of agreement. "In order to counter this, you must do what you were going to do anyway, and continue to do good works, live by faith, and strive toward righteousness in all things. As you do, as more of the force acting in opposition to you attaches itself to you, its lightness will counter the weight of God's hand upon you. In order to avoid being painfully immobilized and destroyed by either the lightness trying to disintegrate you or the gravity of God's hand upon you, friend, you must always strive to balance the two." Kytali paused briefly, but no questions interrupted. "Passivity is not an option for you any longer. Unfortunately, due to the tenuous connection between your material body and the dark matter that now sustains your coherence, you must be diligent in replacing its sanctifying force before it has a chance to erode away. Likewise, because the degree of lightness that needs to be offset cannot be directly correlated to a particular quantity of transubstantiated grain and the relative lightness of any good work or period of humility or such cannot be predicted, you will never be able to cease your good works or your consumption of transubstantiated grain as long as you remain on the righteous path."

"The alternative is much easier, friend, though you may not like the cost." Tarmawy hadn't seen that there was much of an actual cost to following the path of righteousness beyond an enforced commitment to seek the good for the rest of his life, a commitment he had already made, but he didn't question his teachers' statements verbally. Styr'mi continued, "Balance between the physical forces is relatively simple to maintain with manipulation of your spiritual balance in the Market of Souls."

"Yes, that is the other path. The difficulty presented in the former example of balancing purity of character, goodly works and the terrible lightness and instability they bring with the assimilation of the gravity and stability provided by God's hand is largely a symptom of a rigorous dedication to purity. Most Cha Kwytź are not strong enough to follow that path, and even among those who choose it, many fail. The alternative is to do evil in proportion to any overflow of good beyond the extent to which your acceptance of God's hand can sustain."

"You don't actually have to do evil things," Styr'mi corrected, "you can relieve others' souls of the evil in their lives by trading for it."

"Yes, but on the day of judgement we will all be measured by the balance shown in the great Ka'shyk Rěal, and any good or evil we have bought, sold, and traded will stand on possession, as it is written. Whether the righteousness written on one's soul was their own or bought from others, in the end it will be as though it were their own. And the evil deeds that stain the balance sheet of the soul will stand as one's own deeds on that day, whether they committed them or merely accepted them from another. That is the true cost of the other path. You can maintain balance between light and darkness, between lightness and heaviness, with significantly less personal dedication and investment in increasingly beneficent activities, simply by accepting less than purity. By giving up on whole sanctification and ultimate reward. That is the cost."

Tarmawy nodded, still silent.

"Much of the trade that transpires in the Market of Souls, as you have probably already seen if you have put a close eye to its activity, is for the benefit of the Cha Kwytź acting ostensibly as mere brokers to the trade between various Dō Kwytź. Selling their excess good deeds, buying up others' evil, it allows them to keep themselves balanced without having to face as much of the ever-escalating pressure of transforming yourself with God's hand. The challenge of whole sanctification, continual righteousness, and faith without doubt is removed from their shoulders. Many find that to be a significantly easier path. Some find it more difficult to give up virtue and their chance for ultimate reward, and attempt the righteous path. Some of those few eventually find themselves in line to become Ka Kwytź."

Tarmawy politely shifted his pose from that of student, receiving to that of student, inquiring, but waited for Kytali to change his stance appropriately before speaking. "I am already on the path to righteousness. I hope to keep my journey on this path until judgement or death, whichever seeks me first. To live my life according to faith and to virtuous conduct. I do not understand what the challenge or cost to a Cha Kwytź on this path is that makes sacrificing ultimate reward seem worthwhile. Have I missed something? Is there something beyond steadfast adherence required?" His pose shifted back to that of student, receiving as soon as his question had been raised.

"Nothing beyond that, no, but a very difficult balancing the longer that path is followed. Right now, the amount of good you can still do after you first feel an imbalance -as you did tonight- and the amount of time before the force of the imbalance incapacitates or destroys you represents a large margin for you. The amount of transubstantiated grain you need to integrate into your body to regain your health is relatively small, and the unavoidable swing into imbalance in the other direction is proportional and smaller. As time passes and this balancing act is carried out over and over, the effects multiply and compress. You'll have less time after you first feel lightness and pain coming over you to address it, and any good done on the way will reduce that time further for all future occurrences. The amount of dark matter you'll have to assimilate will increase geometrically, and while the margin for error will reduce, the consequence of consuming too much will become greater still. Like a seesaw growing shorter and shorter and bearing more and more weight on both sides with every swing back and forth, the balancing itself becomes unimaginably unreasonable and the scale and impact of good works required to maintain it follows in equal measure."

Another shift of posture, and its acknowledgement, then, "What is the consequence of losing balance or being unable to do enough good in the world?"

"That depends on which side of the scale you happen to be on when collapse comes. If your purity and goodness outstrip your sanctification with dark matter, you'll be torn apart at a molecular scale by the repellent force anchored to every atom of your being. In effect, you will rapidly disintegrate into your component elements and those elemental particles will be immune to the orderly guiding of God's hand, never to bond again. Spiritually, this separates you literally from God for eternity. If instead you incorporate too much of God's hand into your being, one of two things will happen. The more likely thing is that the effective gravity of the dark matter attached to you will be enough to kill you, perhaps even enough to crush you into a dense blue ball of dead flesh. You have certainly attended the consecration of a Cha Kwytź who has died in this way to their home Temple's Listening Singularity, I assume?" Tarmawy nodded assent. "The less likely thing is that you will maintain your balance while striving so stringently toward sanctification that your body's effective gravity will exceed the strength required to bestow upon you the blessing of becoming a singularity yourself. The founding of any new Temple requires the sacrifice of one of our most righteous Cha Kwytź. It also requires careful planning and months of preparations so that the singularity their collapse creates is stabilized to become the new Temple's Listening Singularity. Without the proper rituals -if their collapse was accidental rather than planned- they would become unstuck in space and may even evaporate within seconds. So it is a difficult balance to keep, it requires ever more grand and far-reaching benevolence, piety of character, and unquestioning faith, but the reward is both enabling of the spread of the Kwytzwik and is a personal, singular transformation into the purest expression of sanctity and adherence to God's will available."

"Have you got any questions for us?"

Tarmawy looked from Kytali to Styr'mi and back again, then repeated the motion a few times to indicate dissent.

. • ● ● • .

"That can't be the whole truth, friend."

"Which is what I thought, when I tried to reconcile the options they were giving me with my decades of experience." Tarmawy was meeting in private with friends from his old college study group; they'd all remained close through the years, even as their lives and circumstances had changed. "Nothing they said contradicted what I already knew, but I can't shake the feeling there's more. That there's yet another layer of truth they're waiting to reveal until I've already crossed the point beyond turning back."

"You have to admit, it's an excellent way to maintain secrecy while ensuring participation. They don't tell you what the cost is until after they've already got you eating the transubstantiated grain, and then it's too late. By then you've already reached a point in your walk where your life is at risk unless you go along with everything they're selling." Then, as though to balance his own statement, Mytkin added, "Congratulations, by the way, on becoming Cha Kwytź. Most of us don't have any hope of ascending to that level."

"Thanks, friend. It is certainly a mixed blessing."

"Aren't you worried that discussing this with us is less than righteous behavior? Have you chosen the easier path?" Pwyt'ir sounded genuinely concerned.

"Oh, no, talking to you about this isn't a sin. Look at me, you can see into my Cha'shyk Rěal, you can see that this isn't wrong." Tarmawy hadn't been without a doubt about his choice to go to his friends, but had known it was what he needed to do. "They tried to tell me I should speak only to other Cha Kwytź about it; that they were the only ones who could answer my questions and that revealing all the details to any Dō Kwytź would endanger both of us. I'm not as gullible as Styr'mi, the Cha Kwytź they assigned to me weeks ago, probably when they saw I was approaching a point of pain."

"You don't suppose they could have warned you, do you?" Pwyt'ir said with a tone of concern, "Or explained your options before you were already in pain?"

"Oh, I'm sure they could have, but they wanted to get me hooked. I had to be in a state where rejecting their solution and their explanations was impossible. Styr'mi has been encouraging me to do more lately, and looking back I think some of the opportunities to help people he's brought to my attention were manufactured to get me there quicker. To bring on the pain they wanted to rescue me from as hard and as fast as they could get me to help people in need."

"That's awful." Metaw tended toward brevity.

"But also easy to cover up," Mytkin added, "since even with the despicable intention of getting you to put yourself into unspeakable pain, the act of suggesting that you do more to help people wouldn't be a visible darkness in their Cha'shyk Rěal."

"If this Styr'mi is as gullible as he sounds," suggested Krywit, speaking up for the first time, "it's even possible that he doesn't see that there's anything nefarious or duplicitous about it at all. There's probably someone else--"

"Kytali," interjected Mytkin.

"Yes, possibly Kytali, who was handing down instructions and suggestions to Styr'mi. He could be just as manipulated as you feel right now, friend."

"It's possible. Intelligence is certainly not a prerequisite to religious fervency."

"Any idiot can chant, and some Cha Kwytź don't seem to do much more than that." Krywit sounded bitter, and the others understood why.

"Well, I seem to have become Cha Kwytź despite myself," said Tarmawy, hoping to steer the conversation back toward his current dilemma, "and I'm not ready to give up striving toward virtue just yet, but I don't want to go any further in ignorance. I'm hoping we can work together to figure out or to find out what they're still keeping from me. We uncovered corruption in the university's bureaucracy, we've solved countless puzzles and unraveled mysteries to win cash and prizes. I think that if we apply ourselves and keep our heads down so we don't attract the wrong sort of attention, we can unravel this one, as well."

"You have more access than any of us to the inner workings of the Temple now, friend. How could the rest of us help?"

"You know as well as any of us that six minds working together can see solutions that no individual mind would find, friend." Tarmawy's encouraging spirit was always needed to help the meek Sni'da feel he had anything to offer the group. Sni'da had trouble acknowledging his own unique talent for seeing beyond the obvious to the underlying questions of a mystery. "We would never have found the third golden egg in time if you hadn't realized that every other reference to time in the riddles was actually a reference to distance. The rest of us were trying to calculate celestial dynamics to fit the timing, and you saw the time-space connection. I'm sure there are ways you'll be able to help without personal Cha Kwytź access to the Temple's secrets."

"And I'm sure that even as Cha Kwytź, you won't find the answers simply by looking around or asking at the Temple," said Mytkin, "not until they're ready for you to know."

"I do hope we can figure it out before that," said Pwyt'ir, "I wouldn't want you to be put through an even worse torture before they'll reveal another layer of secrets to you."

"It's possible there isn't any more to it," suggested Mytkin, "that they've already told you everything."

"What about Ka Kwytź?" Metaw asked.

Tarmawy thought for a moment, then said, "Well, they said that the righteous path was the one that might lead to finding oneself in line to be Ka Kwytź. I don't recall any other mention, except using the example of the light of his Cha'shyk Rěal to explain the lightness of being associated with being virtuous. Why?"

"How much dark matter do you suppose Ka Kwytź must assimilate daily to keep up with the scale of his good works?"

"Well," answered Tarmawy, "these are the figures they gave me. The chart doesn't cover that level of activity, but I bet we could..."

"I was looking at it while you were talking earlier," said Sni'da, holding up his notebook to show everyone his notes. "I think a few of these figures are intentionally skewed to encourage you to consume too much grain. They want you to be out of balance. I've sketched out a more accurate curve, here, and with a little more data from your first-hand experience, we can fine tune the formula, here, and probably simplify the calculation." He passed the notebook around, and everyone took a moment to look over his figures.

"What about Ka Kwytź, though?"

Sni'da waited until the notebook returned to him, turned the page, and showed them a few other figures. "I thought it might be interesting to extrapolate out for miracles and the creation of the universe. Based on my calculations, a super-dense star needs to go supernova to create enough gravity to counteract the expansive force predicted by this chart for a miracle on the scale of the eight plagues or even a single resurrection. The creation of the material universe itself was so miraculous that nothing less than the full quantity of dark matter known to be in the universe would have enough gravity to balance such an act, which corresponds nicely with what they were telling you about dark matter."

Krywit grumbled somewhat, put off by Sni'da's ability to entirely fail to stay on topic. "And the actions of Ka Kwytź? How much of the transubstantiated grain would he have to eat every day to keep from disintegrating?"

"Oh, right, uhh..." Sni'da flipped back and forth between several pages of notes he'd quickly sketched out, looking for the relevant figures, "somewhere in the neighborhood of fifty to eighty kiloliters. Depending on the season, and how busy he is on a particular day, of course."

"Wait, what? How much?"

"Well, because of the balance issues he must be experiencing, operating at that level, certainly not less than fifty thousand liters of the grain," repeated Sni'da.

The others just stared at him, wide-eyed. They knew his math would prove out, but saw what Sni'da could not see about what he had just said. Metaw said what the others were thinking, "He must use something else."

"What?"

Tarmawy explained the obvious fact which Sni'da could not see on his own, "Ka Kwytź could not physically consume and digest that much grain, friend. Most Kwytzwik would be hard-pressed to consume more than two liters' worth of food in a day without getting sick. Fifty thousand liters of grain would keep the average Kwytzwik feeling overfed for about a century, even without the extra heaviness of the transubstantiated grain. There's no way he could ingest that much every day."

"Oh," said Sni'da, "yeah."

"Yeah. So..." Mytkin wondered, verbally, "that's one thing they aren't telling you, yet... What else..."

"Well, what about the Listening Singularities? Did anyone else know they were dead Cha Kwytź?" Pwyt'ir asked, "Does it seem strange to anyone else that we confess to Cha Kwytź who were so sanctified that they collapsed into tiny black holes?"

"The philosophical basis for it is still sound," said Krywit. "Your secrets and confessions, even if somehow they were heard by the Cha Kwytź who'd formed the singularity, still couldn't ever escape the event horizon. It's a one-way communication that only God -and apparently the very godly few whose sacrifice provides us the conduit- could have access to. The Listening Singularity, even if it used to be just another Kwytzwik, can only listen. It can only keep your secret between you and God, it can never share it."

"Sure, but what else aren't they telling us about it, and why don't they reveal even the basics until you become Cha Kwytź? I can see how it makes sense to reveal the gravitic nature at the heart of all our beliefs at the same time they begin literally feeding you gravity, but why not reveal it to the rest of the Kwytzwik? If God's presence in the universe is seen as dark energy, which we can only infer by examining missing gravity, and God's interaction with the universe is through the gravity of dark matter, wouldn't confessing into the gravity well of a singularity make more sense within that larger context?"

"That's certainly something to investigate. Why do we have one religion for the masses and a more understandable, more detailed version of the same religion for the select few?"

"Because it's a religion universal to all Kwytzwik," said Sni'da, "by virtue of being Kwytzwik. And because it isn't universal, too, in that no non-Kwytzwik can follow it."

"You're saying they aren't under pressure to make our beliefs comprehensible or easy to understand, because we're a captive audience?"

Krywit answered before Sni'da could come up with a response. "They're obviously holding back the facts so that faith seems mysterious and inscrutable. They only want blind adherents to reach the level of Cha Kwytź, and having an easily comprehensible set of beliefs that was all tied together by concepts backed up by science would bring too many intelligent, informed citizens up the ranks. They want Cha Kwytź like Styr'mi, not like Tarmawy."

"That might explain why Kytali was so unfriendly toward me," conjectured Tarmawy. "I thought it was just his personality, or his attempt to come across as a stern teacher, but perhaps he was letting his distrust of my well-known intellectual curiosity come through. I certainly didn't want to question anything he had to say at the time."

"Of course, here you are getting us started trying to unravel further mysteries about the faith," said Mytkin. "I suppose you don't want to be discovered investigating any of this, do you?"

"No. Who knows what measures they might go to if they thought I was a threat? We'll have to keep quiet about this. Spread out and do most of our investigations in other towns and other Temples."

"Most Cha Kwytź aren't going to be forthcoming with details, regardless of our location. It's possible that most Cha Kwytź don't know any more than you do." Krywit was sceptical.

"And we don't really know what we're looking for," added Pwyt'ir, "aside from information about how the Ka Kwytź can survive. He isn't doing it by eating transubstantiated grain, that's for sure."

"Well," concluded Mytkin, "this looks to be quite a challenge, then, doesn't it?"

. • ● ● • .

Krywit was on his way back from interviewing a retired foreman, a bounty of information in his head and a bounty of a strangely light material in his pack, when a black, windowless van pulled up beside him. The door was opened before it stopped, three large, masked figures pulled Krywit inside, covering his mouth and restraining his limbs, and then the van was in motion again almost before his feet were off the ground. The door slammed shut as Krywit found himself shoved to the floor of the van by the frightening figures who had kidnapped him.

"What did the old man tell you?" One of the large men shouted at him.

"I don't," Krywit stuttered, "I don't know what you're talking about!"

Another of the men hit him hard across the face.

"We've been following you. We know you aren't doing research for school, you graduated years ago.

Tell us what we want to know!" Another hard strike to the face.

"You can't, you, you, you, you can't do this!" Krywit could feel himself reverting back to the old familiar role the Cha Kwytź at primary school had worked so hard to keep him in. He could hear himself turning back into that weak, stuttering coward he had sworn he would never be again. Krywit tried to muster enough strength of will to hold his own. "You can't do this to me! I have rights!"

The van turned hard, tires squealing, and he felt himself sliding toward the back of the van. Another masked figure, who had been silent and non-violent up to that point in this exchange, was suddenly crouching right over him. "What makes you think you have any rights?" This one was holding what looked like a police baton, and brought it down hard against Krywit's chest. The sound of a rib breaking inside him was unmistakable, even over the van's engine noise. He bit down on his tongue, refusing to cry out. "Now tell us, what did the old man say? Did he give you anything?" Another hit with the baton, right back against the already broken rib, and a pair of hands was trying to pull Krywit's pack from his back. He had to twist onto his side, onto his battered and broken rib cage, to let them take the pack without taking his arm along with it.

"Let's see what he's got in here while he spills the beans," said the one who took the pack. "Go on, talk!"

"I told you, I don't know what you're talking about!" Krywit could taste blood in his mouth, but couldn't feel the pain in his tongue past that in his chest. He held the line. "What old man?"

"There's no use lying to us. We'll find the truth."

"Look-eee-here! What have we got here?" The figure going through Krywit's stolen pack held up the container the old man had given him. "Is this what I think it is? It feels like it!" He tossed the container from hand to hand, feeling it fail to behave as expected.

"I see it's as bad as we thought. What are we going to do with you, now?"

"We can't let him live, not with what he knows." They were talking about him as though he weren't actually there, listening to them.

"We'll have to go back and take care of the old man, too. He's proven he can't be trusted." The van made a U-turn, and everyone in the back was grasping at the walls to avoid being thrown hard into them.

"How do you want to do it?"

"Kill two birds with one stone, I say. Feed that stuff to him. He'll disintegrate. No body, no evidence. The old man's death is easier. He's practically waiting to die as it is."

The one holding the container moved toward the back of the van and handed it to the one who had used the baton. Opening it, he remarked, "That's what I thought. Just a hand full of shavings. Perfect." Then the shavings from the container were being force-fed to Krywit as the van returned to the old man's home.

"Are you sure that'll be enough? What if he survives?"

"He'd have to be an unrepentant war criminal to be that far out of balance. This amount would be enough to destroy you, and I know what you've been up since your last visit to the Market. We've just got to get rid of him before he has a chance to start digesting it."

The driver slammed on the breaks as soon as the dregs of the container were forced down Krywit's throat, and the van's tires squealed as it skidded to a stop. Before he could even cough or sputter over the metal shavings that had been forced into his throat, Krywit had been tossed out into the ditch on the side of the road. The van sped away and was quickly out of sight. He reached into his pocket, which had somehow not been searched by the ruffians who had abducted, beat, and tried to kill him, and retrieved his mobile phone. He hit number one on his speed dial, rolled, wincing, onto his back, and held the phone to his ear.

When his call was answered he said, "It's a good thing I wasn't wearing my Cha'shyk Rěal today, or I might already be dead."

. • ● ● • .

"This is the key, then." Mytkin was watching as Tarmawy wrapped bandages around Krywit's body. "Exotic matter, the innermost chamber, and whatever secret lays inside it. We're finally making some real headway on this thing, but at what cost?"

"I'm not dead yet," said Krywit.

"We don't know how long you'll last, though." Pwyt'ir held his hand.

"As far as I'm concerned, it's been long enough already." He winced in pain, as even Tarmawy's gentle touch was too much for his tortured torso. "I lived long enough to tell the rest of you what I learned. To tell you that they're watching, and that they're willing to kill to protect the secret."

"There's no harm in killing, since they're working for Cha Kwytź who are in on it. They can just transfer the sin to Cha Kwytź who need it to stay balanced on the easy path."

"Sure," said Tarmawy, "they practically require Dō Kwytź to go on sinning in order to live. I don't think I could ever walk that path."

"Well whether or not this ends up killing me, I don't want to see any of the rest of you to fall into their hands. You've got to arm yourselves. If I'd had some way to protect myself, they might not have been able to destroy the only evidence we had."

"What are you suggesting? That we become as bad as they are?"

"If that's what it takes to find the truth and reveal it."

"We don't even know what the truth is," countered Mytkin. "What if we get to the bottom of things and discover that we agree that the truth should be kept from the people?"

"If that happens," said Tarmawy without looking up from putting the finishing touches on Krywit's bandages, "then we'll already be as bad as they are."

"So what do you suggest?"

"Well, before we start shopping for weapons to defend ourselves, let's try to figure out this new clue. Exotic matter and the innermost chamber. What do we know?"

Sni'da finally spoke up, not looking up from his notebook or ceasing his calculations, "Exotic matter, as we've all just learned, is matter which is like normal matter in every way except that it has a negative mass. Thus, it has a couple of very strange properties. One, it interacts with matter via gravity in direct opposition to our normal understanding of gravity. Two, it seems also to behave as though the physical laws relating to inertia are reversed. So when it's at rest it wants to be in motion, and when in motion it wants to either speed up, slow down, or stop. Anything but maintaining the same speed."

"How is it killing him?" asked Pwyt'ir.

"Oh, that's the first property. Since it's matter with a negative mass, feeding it to him was like the opposite of feeding him transubstantiated grain. Well, except that where the grain merely has dark matter anchored to its own standard material existence, the exotic matter itself embodies the reversed gravity effects and thus does not suffer the same deleterious effects over time that the grain does. Nor does its effective lightness merely represent a transient property of the relative lightness of his soul, but rather a permanent lightness that..." Sni'da looked up from his double-checked calculations, "his body won't be able to rid itself of."

"What does all that mean?"

"It's as though he suddenly did more good in one day than the rest of us put together, and even if we could somehow smuggle transubstantiated grain to him it would only be a stop-gap measure. He's as much in danger of falling out of balance as any long-time Cha Kwytź, but without the benefit of years of practice at maintaining that balance, doing good works, or leading a pious life. In fact, if not for the childhood transgression that has haunted his entire life and made him a second-class citizen, he would have been significantly out of balance within a few minutes' digestion." Sni'da held up a page of figures none of them could understand at a glance, saying, "based on these calculations, if he does anything so good as helping an elder across a busy street, he'll evaporate -or maybe just explode- within seconds."

Pwyt'ir released Krywit's hand and stepped back.

"We should gift him our sin." Metaw looked to Tarmawy. Tarmawy furrowed his brow.

"I suppose we could, if we had his permission. I've been taught the chants to intone for that. It has to be a direct person to person transfer, though. Taking on everyone's sin to transfer it to him at once would put me too far out of balance. It means sixty percent more intonations and a lot more patience on Krywit's part, but you can't exactly go to the Temple and ask half a dozen Cha Kwytź in the Market of Souls to transfer everything simultaneously. They'd know you were up to something."

"I can take it," volunteered Krywit, in a weak voice. "And at this point I'm pretty well used to having a black Cha'shyk Rěal. If bearing my friends' sin saves my life and brings us closer to unraveling this mystery, I'll bear it."

"That's very noble of you," said Pwyt'ir, still backing away slowly.

"I guess we should get started, then. Who wants to go first?"

. • ● ● . .

Dressed head to toe in black, every inch of their blue skin covered with leather, cloth, or black paint, their identities were hidden. Not even that they were Kwytzwik could be confirmed or denied by looking at them, even going so far as to wear head coverings which obfuscated their hairless heads and their pointed ears. They were armed only with hard to handle swords, and none of the five felt they had enough practice yet at wielding them. Their best defense was that they were going to make their first attempt to breach the inner chamber of the Temple when its population was the lowest; there would be fewer Kwytzwik to witness the act and fewer Cha Kwytź to try to stop them. They didn't know what they would find if they succeeded, only that they had invested so much by then that they simply couldn't give up.

The five figures, dressed dark as shadow and clothed in the darkness of night, approached the Kwytzwik Temple in a town almost as far from their home town as one could go before exceeding the reach of the Kwytzwik. Krywit could not join them. He had not been out of bed since the day of his brief abduction. Partially so that those who believed him to be dead would not see him alive, but more because even with as much weight of sin as the six of them could lay upon him, the exotic matter was still tearing him apart. The others did not hesitate as they entered the Temple, remembering the destroyed life of their friend.

As they passed by the prayer stalls, only a single Kwytzwik was present and she did not look up to see who was passing behind her. She remained focused -as she should be- on her fervent prayers. As they came around and into view of the Market of Souls, three of the five friends felt relief that there were only a handful of Kwytzwik there. The other two remained tense, ready to draw their swords if they faced any resistance. That night, they faced only confused stares from the Dō Kwytź, and the Cha Kwytź chanting over them did not drop even a single syllable as the masked figures passed by. They passed by the Sanctification Waterfall and the Listening Singularity of the Temple, knowing more about their secrets than most Kwytzwik ever learn, and proceeded into the sanctuary that was the final arc of the spiral-shape wrapping the building around the glowing sphere at its core.

The sphere was the barrier separating them from the inner chamber. It glowed, golden, and seemed not to have a definitive edge. Tarmawy, at the head of the group, drew his sword and pointed it at the wall of light that was an entrance only Ka Kwytź could cross. He pressed the point of the sword forward, into the light. There was resistance, but like pressing fruit into a gelatin, it seemed to be a misleading and ephemeral resistance. The sword penetrated the wall of light with unexpected ease. It penetrated the light, and the light dimmed somewhat. The others stepped forward with their swords drawn and waited to see what would happen.

Tarmawy tried to slice down, through the barrier with his sword, but instead of leaving an open gash it passed through the barrier as through a liquid which flowed together in its wake. There was little more than a slight trail of dimness to show where his sword had cut through the barrier. He pulled the sword back out.

One of the others gasped at the sight of it. Ahead of the point past which he had not inserted the blade into the light, the unbelievably expensive metal it had been formed from had apparently been eaten away at by the barrier. There was hardly more than a whisper of the blade's former strength left where it had been put to use. He tried pressing what was left of it back into the light and quickly pulled back what appeared to be a blade broken off mere inches from the hilt. They all stood, staring, unsure as to the meaning of the missing sword, until one of them pointed out that where the light had gone dim in the sword's passing path, it was already recovering its brilliance.

Another of them pressed their sword into the barrier and felt with diminishing amazement the diminishing size of the blade as he swept it up and down in the path the first sword had drawn. When the second sword had been consumed, the line which had been only faintly dimmer than the surrounding light was now noticeably darker, a clearly visible effect. One by one the five of them tried their hand at cutting their way into the barrier, and one by one their swords disappeared into the light. When the last of their swords was gone there was a thin breach, barely a slit, through which they could see into the inner chamber for a few seconds before it started to seal itself back up.

Without a single word passing between them since they'd arrived, after watching the golden light restore itself to its former solidity, they turned around and walked out of the Temple. The Cha Kwytź in the Market of Souls still gave them no reaction. The woman praying a littler further on had not yet lifted her head from the floor, and still did not deviate from the requirements of ritual prayer as they passed. The night stood just as dark and silent as it had been before, and they walked out into it, five figures carrying five hilts without swords in their hands.

. • ● ● • .

"I think we're going to have to rob a bank or two." Mytkin had been doing figures in his head. "Getting together enough exotic matter to form five rapiers cost us each over a years' wages. In order to actually get us in to the inner chamber, I figure we'll need to clear out the vaults at a couple of banks to afford enough exotic matter to do the job."

"We may as well," said Pwyt'ir, "we won't be able to keep Krywit alive much longer without some pretty hefty sins under our belts."

"We just have to keep him alive until our private crop of sanctified grain is ready for harvest, and then keeping him alive will be much easier." Tarmawy was hopeful, though he realized that with the dismal result of their first attempt to breach the inner chamber of a Temple, their chances weren't very good.

"You saw the same thing in there as we did, friend. The time for trying to solve this mystery without sacrificing the path of righteousness is past. You've got to be all in."

"You think I'm not as dedicated to this as the rest of you?"

"You didn't put up as much capital as the rest of us, that's for sure. The only one who chipped in less was Krywit, and he's been effectively dead for the last year and a half."

"Cha Kwytź aren't exactly wealthy, you know. Poverty is one of the virtues I've got to maintain in order to stay balanced."

"If you'd just taken the easy path, you'd have a lot less difficulty keeping balanced and you'd be as wealthy as any other Cha Kwytź who participates in the Market properly."

"They're part of the problem! What do you think we're fighting against? Greed, corruption, and lies fed to Dō Kwytź by the very Cha Kwytź you seem to want me to emulate to make your life easier! None of you would even be aware of this stuff if I hadn't brought it to you in the first place."

"I'm beginning to think it might have been better if you hadn't, friend."

There was a long, tense silence after that, as they scowled and fumed at each other. Finally, Krywit spoke up in the small voice he had left. "I'm the one who gets to decide if this venture has been worthwhile, as I'm the one paying the highest price for it. When one of you dies at their hands, you can try to have a say about it, but until then, please just take my word for it that this is the most important thing any of us will ever do with our lives." He coughed roughly, clearly in pain, and then continued. "Money doesn't matter, your reputations don't matter, and even the possibility of ultimate reward for one among us is not as important as the greater good of all Kwytzwik. If Sni'da is right about what you saw in there, then a great injustice is being done to the most righteous among us, and it is being done on behalf of all of us without our knowledge or consent. Something must be done." He'd tried to finish with strength of conviction in his voice, but doubled up in another coughing fit as soon as he finished speaking. Pwyt'ir fetched him a fresh glass of water.

"If we have to rob banks, we have to rob banks, but we're going to need something more effective than those swords at penetrating the entrance to the inner chamber."

"I've been thinking about that," Sni'da again was working out abstract functions by hand in the notebook he seemed always to have with him, "and I think I may have a solution. Based on my observations, it seemed that the exotic matter had the greatest effect on diminishing the barrier and the light it gave off while in motion through it. By postulating that this has to do with kinetic energy amplifying the force of gravity exerted against the energy field by the inverse mass of the exotic matter, I project that we simply need to accelerate our incursions to improve our effectiveness."

"Bullets instead of blades," clarified Metaw.

"Exactly," confirmed Sni'da.

"Bullets? I could barely swing a sword of that stuff in a straight line," countered Mytkin. "What makes you think bullets would go where we wanted them?"

"Well, I'm not as worried about them changing direction," said Sni'da, "as I am about them changing speed. Negative mass means inverse inertia means they accelerate at random rates pretty much continuously. Some of them would hit their target at speeds far in excess of the force applied to them while others would slow down or perhaps reverse direction."

"You want us to shoot the entrance to the inner chamber with bullets that cost more than I earn in a year, and you're telling me they may turn around in midair and come flying back at us?"

"Yes." Sni'da seemed certain. "Unless you can think of another easy way to accelerate exotic matter up to high speeds and force it into the barrier."

"Of course, walking into a Temple carrying firearms is somewhat different from walking in with a sword strapped to your back. It seems we'd be more likely to face opposition that way."

"Well, we would be armed, just as we were with the swords... On our way in, I mean."

"Not really. We can't exactly go firing our exotic matter bullets into whoever tries to stand in our way. We'll need every ounce of the stuff just to get into the inner chamber."

"So what do you suggest we use, instead?"

"The sword smith who made our swords was telling me about something that would probably do well to keep anyone from even thinking of getting in our way, on intimidation alone. He called it an Unholy Lightning Sword."

. • ● ● • .

The crackle of the black lightning which danced eternally up and down each Unholy Lightning Sword was, in fact, intimidating enough that they only had to strike someone down once on a bank job. Most people just stayed out of their way when they walked into a bank with Unholy Lightning Swords drawn. Tellers handed over the contents of bank vaults without a hint of resistance.

One bank's nervous guard had accidentally discharged his firearm at them and, as advertised, the Unholy Lightning greedily leapt from Mytkin's sword and consumed the metal projectile before it could do any damage.

One bank's silent alarm was tripped as the five of them, completely hidden in their black disguises, had entered a particularly high profile bank. After they'd collected the contents of the vault, they stepped outside to find themselves surrounded by what appeared to be every police officer the foreign city had to offer. Their haul in packs on their backs, their Unholy Lightning Swords at the ready, the five of them walked out without paying heed to the bullhorn-enhanced shouting of the police officers. A rain of bullets was unleashed upon them, and though they knew it was unnecessary, they spun and flourished the blades in the air to put on a show for the audience of assembled constabulary. Unholy Lightning arced out to each bullet fired upon them without regard to their number, and the five masked thieves advanced steadily, unfazed. Eventually the police ran out of bullets, and the unharmed state of the five thieves put a terror in them that left the masked Kwytzwik unchallenged as they disappeared from the scene.

Accumulating the vast wealth required to purchase and weaponize enough exotic matter to breach the inner chamber of a Temple generated nearly enough sin to keep Krywit in balance while things were coming together. They worked with non-Kwytzwik for nearly everything they needed, trying to keep a low profile among their own. Tarmawy kept up appearances at their local Temple and kept his ears peaked for any word that might have put their first attempt on a Temple together with all their bank jobs, but no such word came. Word had certainly spread through the international press and speculation was certainly rampant across the FÆ about the masked thieves who robbed banks all over the globe wielding Unholy Lightning Swords. Not even the most outlandish suggestions had come close to their true identities and motives.

When the time finally came that they were ready to attempt to breach another Temple, it was with significantly less doubt than they'd felt before their first try. They had each spent enough hours practicing with their Unholy Lightning Swords that they could have taken on all but the most experienced sword fighters in single combat. They were confident in their ability. They had each spent over a hundred hours learning to shoot straight, and then almost as much again learning to handle their custom-built automatic weapons and to get used to the exotic bullets they fired. After the first day of shooting the most expensive bullets ever crafted, they'd all also begun practicing catching the odd, unpredictable bullets in butterfly nets woven from titanium wire. They felt sure they were ready for anything.

They were also possessed of a fairly negative view of what the upper echelons of the Kwytzwik clergy had become and how that translated down to all the Dō Kwytź under their sway. They walked into the Temple they had selected ready to do whatever it took to reach their goal. Desensitized to the price of sin, confident in the corruption of Cha Kwytź, and certain they would discover even darker truths when they finally reached the inner chamber, they marched in. An innocent Dō

Kwytź on his way out from one of the prayer stalls saw the five masked thieves brandishing Unholy Lightning Swords, knew immediately that they were the ones who had been robbing banks worldwide, and stood in their way as though to protect the Temple. The Dō Kwytź planted their feet, spread out their arms, and blocked Pwyt'ir from proceeding.

Pwyt'ir hesitated.

Metaw, coming up behind him, did not.

The Dō Kwytź, suddenly short an arm, fell to the ground. Metaw stepped over the trembling, crying body, and Pwyt'ir followed.

They didn't run into any more resistance until they reached the more busy passage of the Market of Souls. A Dō Kwytź waiting his turn to buy a little virtue saw in the masked thieves an opportunity to actually do good instead of buying someone else's. He walked with a cane, and after the sword-wielding, black-clad figured had passed by, he lifted his cane into the air and brought it down hard across the back of Pwyt'ir's neck. Pwyt'ir knew better than to make a noise or cry out, but turned with a resolute spirit he had not possessed moments earlier.

Pwyt'ir, with two quick slashes of his Unholy Lightning Sword, cut through the cane, across the chest, and then through the legs of the resistant Dō Kwytź. The Unholy Lightning Swords were sharp, but more than that they were hungry, and their victims rarely survived and never were so lucky as to have their limbs reattached. Pwyt'ir turned back around and was back in step with his friends before his victim's body hit the floor.

Another couple of Dō Kwytź, but no Cha Kwytź, tried to stand in their way, stop them, or otherwise dissuade them. They fell as well. The hot, wet spray of lavender blood from one dying Dō Kwytź across the face of a chanting Cha Kwytź did not displace even a single syllable of intonation or a single beat of their careful meter. The masked thieves knew the Cha Kwytź could not risk unplanned good deeds or even strong empathy without the possibility of putting themselves out of balance and their lives on the line. Their selfishness and greed kept them from standing in the way of crime against the Dō Kwytź or against the Temple.

As they passed by the Listening Singularity, Tarmawy -though without descending the stairs to kneel in the proper position- spoke softly into it, "We're on our way." None of them bothered to cleanse themselves in the Sanctification Waterfall. They crossed into the sanctuary and took up positions before the glowing golden sphere that was the entrance to the inner chamber. They sheathed their Unholy Lightning Swords and drew their automatic weapons. Tarmawy, at point, was the first to fire, and soon there were five streams of the strange bullets headed toward the same point on the barrier.

As expected, some of the exotic bullets failed to follow a straight path toward the barrier, and soon there were countless small projectiles variously speeding up and slowing down and floating up instead of falling down and otherwise ricocheting haphazardly around the amphitheater. They were used to this behavior, and did not react. They just kept firing.

The light of the barrier dimmed. They kept firing.

A dark spot, like unto a stain that won't come out in the wash, began to form where their aim was focused. They kept firing.

The barrier's light darkened from golden and glittering to a dirty, murky brown light. They kept firing.

The surface of it began to divide and then to crack open. They kept firing, now two aiming just to the left of the crack and two aiming just to the right of the crack, with Tarmawy firing right into the opening they had made.

The crack widened, broadened, opened to reveal the inner chamber to them. They peered in, but they kept firing. They were the first, other than Ka Kwytź, who had witnessed the inner chamber, and they saw there what they had thought they'd glimpsed when their swords had penetrated the other Temple's inner chamber so many months before. It was exactly as bad as they'd feared.

Tarmawy stopped firing. He dropped his gun to the ground. He stepped toward the widening breach in the darkening wall of light. He genuflected and began to chant. He intoned, with all the strength of will he could muster, the syllables that would reverse the secret ritual which had captured the former Cha Kwytź inside. After he'd given voice to the first stanza, the others ceased firing; they could see that his voice was having more effect than their grossly expensive bullets. They shouldered their guns, pulled out their nets, and began running around the sanctuary retrieving errant exotic matter to the beautiful sound of freedom Tarmawy was singing to the singularity clearly visible inside. No one interrupted.

Around the time the other four had finished gathering stray bullets and reloading their weapons, Tarmawy completed the portion of the ritual they had been able to uncover, hoping it would be enough. What remained of the convex wall of formerly golden light blocking passage into the inner chamber to all but Ka Kwytź was a mere translucent shadow, and more an opening than a barrier to entry. They all stood at the edge of the inner chamber, looking in.

Sni'da was the first to speak. "We were right. They're capturing the dark matter and dark energy the singularity is pulling in so they can feed it into Ka Kwytź. That device there probably serves as storage."

"Which is why Ka Kwytź is always travelling from Temple to Temple," said Mytkin. "He consumes the dark energy collected since his last visit and moves on. Our Temples are harvesting and storing, collectively, just enough dark energy to sustain a single Ka Kwytź. That must be why there's never more than one."

"But the number of Temples is always growing. Shouldn't their capacity be going up at the same rate?" Pwyt'ir was thinking about all the Cha Kwytź who were sanctified enough to become a singularity but who couldn't become Ka Kwytź because there could only be one at a time. "Every time a Cha Kwytź becomes gloriously sanctified to the point that they'd need access to the richer gravity of this dark energy, a new Temple is built on their grave."

They all paused for a moment, realizing more clearly that they were looking at the final resting place of some unknown Cha Kwytź. Careful planning had brought them prepared. Tarmawy stayed back, not wanting to accidentally trigger the device and end up overwhelmed with dark energy he wasn't prepared to take on, but the other four advanced into the inner chamber. Tarmawy picked up and shouldered his gun while the others began setting up their equipment. It took a relatively long time to configure, as they hadn't known for certain how the inner chamber would be laid out. They'd accurately predicted the angle and location of the long funnel that from the other end was known as the Listening Singularity, its exotic matter sheath the clue that had put Krywit on his death bed and led them finally to the heart of the mystery. Obtaining and learning to operate this final piece of equipment had been the most difficult to do in secret.

They double-checked all the details, every connection and alignment, and switched the equipment on. Then the four of them kneeled before the singularity now surrounded by apparatus and began to pray. Tarmawy genuflected again, just outside the chamber, and began to chant a prayer along with them. They could hear the equipment warming up, the sound of energy building within it, and they raised their voices over it.

Everyone for miles around heard a loud pop as the singularity became unstuck. Less dramatically, everyone in and near the Temple heard a crack, like thunder, as the equipment fired, seconds later.

Tarmawy's chant changed. The other four stood and began quickly to disassemble the now quite hot equipment from around the new singularity it had created at the center of the chamber. The barely visible shadow of the barrier began to solidify again, and to brighten as Tarmawy intoned the ritual usually used to capture sanctified Cha Kwytź. There was just enough time to break down the equipment and leap out of the inner chamber before the breach was too small to pass through, and soon the golden light was restored to its former glorious, unbroken brilliance. When they left the Temple, they met no resistance and saw no trace of their earlier violence.

. • ● ● • .

"How many Temples are there in the world?"

"Does it really make a difference," asked Tarmawy, "if we can make the world a better place by breaking in to every one?"

"How much is this going to cost?"

"In terms of life," asked Sni'da, "or in terms of money?" He was already working on calculations to extrapolate both for the remaining Temples.

"Couldn't we petition Ka Kwytź to do it as he makes his rounds?" Pwyt'ir asked, stating, "he still gets his dark energy, plus he doesn't have to rob banks to afford to get into the inner chamber; he can just walk in any time he likes."

"I doubt Ka Kwytź would go along with that. He's old guard, and strongly dedicated to upholding tradition," explained Tarmawy. "I petitioned him for a meeting early last year and as of this morning the request hasn't even made it through all the layers of bureaucracy between myself, a relatively new Cha Kwytź, and Ka Kwytź. It's not like we could just send him fæ-mail. If he won't give up a thousand-year-old chain of command to enable communication among the clergy, what makes you think Ka Kwytź would accept the sort of radical shift we want to suggest?"

"But it's the right thing to do," argued Mytkin. "Those Cha Kwytź earned their gravity through hard work, unwavering faith, and sanctification on a grand scale. Keeping to tradition means stealing their reward, and separating them from God!"

"They aren't entirely separated from God, friend. A certain amount of dark energy is able to flow to them via the narrow path that turns them into Listening Singularities rather than mere gravity traps for Ka Kwytź to feed upon." Pwyt'ir hadn't been the same since he'd killed another Kwytzwik, despite the sin being transferred to a very grateful Krywit. "I'm sure that's how Cha Kwytź in the know and Ka Kwytź justify their crimes to themselves. They haven't condemned Cha Kwytź to the Hell of total separation from God, they've merely subverted the communion with God due them so Ka Kwytź can bask in the stored and multiplied presence of God."

"You know as well as any of us that the funnel reveals less than a single degree's worth of the singularity's spherical event horizon to the universe," said Sni'da, "and that the rest of their potential connection with God is blocked by the barrier."

"I know, I know, but there are only five of us to fix it, and there are thousands of Temples, thousands of trapped Cha Kwytź being cut off from God."

"Then it's our duty to release as many of them as we're able." Tarmawy was resolute.

"By my calculation, there isn't enough wealth in the world to buy enough exotic matter at a fair price to breach every Temple," said Sni'da. "And there isn't enough exotic matter being discovered and manufactured in the world to keep up with the rate at which we'll be using it up."

Metaw responded succinctly. "We'll have to make our own."

The Greater Good

"Really? Hasn't it been, like, eight hundred years since the last of the Triskelion opposition was defeated? I'd have thought this would have happened back then if the prophecies were being correctly interpreted."

"You know the scriptures, right?"

"Of course. Doesn't everybody?"

"Sure, but we each interpret scripture individually. Think about the prophecies. They said the desolation of the Triskelion abomination from the Earth would only come when the generation of opposition had passed away."

"Which they did, eight centuries ago."

"But it didn't say how soon after the generation had passed away it would happen. Think about the other parts of the prophecy that said that no one would know the day or the hour of desolation. Or look at it this way; there's the part where it says that when the time of desolation comes, every Triskelion everywhere on Earth would know at once that the time had come. It says that the sign would be made by a loud noise and a bright light from across the sky. Isn't that a scriptural description of television? Sound and light sent across the sky so that people everywhere will know the good news at once?"

"I guess so..."

"Don't tell me you aren't ready to give up this parasitic existence and leave the world in peace."

"If I weren't, I'd be the opposition myself, wouldn't I? Then the whole thing would have to start over."

"Not necessarily; you'd just have to die before the rest of us."

"Which, if I were in opposition, I wouldn't want to do. Wasn't that the entire point of opposition? Claiming some sort of bizarre right to life?"

"Not just a right to life. Some of them claimed that Triskelions weren't an abomination. The opposition philosopher Klume went as far as to claim that we represented a unique beauty that deserved to be preserved and protected."

"Beauty? Triskelions? Was Klume blind, deaf and dumb?"

"Two out of three, yes. He claimed that his blindness allowed him to see the true beauty of our place in the world. Clearly, he was dumb to believe his own twisted rhetoric."

"I didn't mean dumb as in stupid, I meant--"

"I know, I know. And Klume would have been better off if he hadn't been able to speak. He became an outcast, lost the protection of the elders, and was killed by Danitoreans the way we all deserve to be; mercilessly."

"Good for him. I know I hope and pray daily to be half as lucky as that. If this is for real, maybe I'll finally be allowed to be killed."

"Maybe we all will be."

. • ● ● • .

"I thought we'd have to go to war. Doesn't the scripture say the Danitoreans will raise an army against us?"

"They are raising an army, but not against us. The Tuvali to the South, and our Celadarian allies across the sea have said they won't allow the Danitoreans to commit genocide against any of their allies, and have committed troops to defend us against the coming desolation."

"Haven't our bishops explained that we've been waiting for this to come to pass for dozens of generations? What part of our abominable existence do they want to see preserved in the world? Even our little children know inherently that Triskelion existence is a cursed one, and a blight on the land. Why else would mortality rates be so high among our offspring too young to know better than to kill themselves?"

"I know this, and you know this, and no matter how vociferously Triskelions try to clarify this to our diplomatic and trade partners, they don't seem to understand us. Of course, true believers can't actually ask for death, so that might be part of the problem."

"Well, sure. If we believed we had a right to death, we'd all have been dead long ago. Just because we all wish we were dead, and we know we deserve to be dead, doesn't mean we believe we have any right to death."

"Oh, you don't have to tell me. Tell the religious fanatics who have been organizing marches all over. Tell the ones who have been picketing the sites where clinics are going up in the capital. They're saying that going along with this peacefully is the same as claiming a right to death."

"How can they say that being killed by those who have the right to do as they please is the same as Triskelions -who have no rights- choosing to die?"

"Well, choosing to go into one of the clinics is the same as choosing death, in a way. So if you believe you have the right to choose to accept what's waiting for you in the clinic, you're saying in effect that you believe you have the right to die. That's their argument, anyway."

"What if the Danitoreans rounded us up, without our individual permission and without warning, and took us to the clinics? I've heard rumor of that as a proposed bureaucratic option the church was considering, to keep such choices out of the hands of the laity."

"As far as I know, that's just a rumor. If the bishops made such a suggestion or consented to such a thing, it would be the same as having the people as a whole choosing death. Our religious leaders are our representatives, so their choices and actions reflect on all Triskelions, before other nations and before God. It would be meaningless to take the choice out of the hands of the laity, if such action had been chosen by the clergy."

"So we have to hope the Danitoreans come up with the idea on their own?"

"I'm pretty sure that as bad as we make life for them, they won't need to be encouraged to do whatever it takes to get rid of us."

"Tell that to all the generations of Triskelions that came before us. Tell that to every Triskelion who wished -for their own sake as well as for the greater good of all- that they could die, but who knew better than to presume that it was their own choice to make. Why didn't the Danitoreans do whatever it took to get rid of us eight hundred years ago, when the last of the opposition was gone?"

"That's not for us to say, and you know it. We aren't supposed to try to understand, we're merely supposed to be Triskelions. To embrace the horrid life we've been given, to be infectious parasites, to disgust not just the Danitoreans and anyone else wise enough to see us for what we are, but to disgust even ourselves with our very existence. It is not our place to question why we live, but to live."

"Of course. I never intended to question the basic tenets of scripture. I just have my doubts about what's happening. I don't feel I deserve to be lucky enough to be a part of the last generation. I don't deserve the privilege of being a part of the desolation. It's hard to believe it could all be true."

"It isn't about you and me, and it isn't about our generation being the lucky one. It's about justice, and balance, and the greater good. Triskelions have existed to be an example of everything wrong and bad, so the world can know what it means to do right and to be good. The opposition embraced that position, but didn't understand that the deeper truth was not that evil ought to exist, to give contrast to good. The deeper truth is what the rest of us know even before we are old enough to understand, and that is that evil ought not to exist."

"But not that evil has the right to remove itself from the world. We have to let the righteous decide to cast aside the wretched. They have to know good well enough and be good enough to no longer need evil around to show them the wrong way. It's just hard for me to believe that the world is good enough, and this generation of Danitoreans righteous enough, that the time for the Triskelion abomination has passed. It seems too good to be true."

"Maybe it is. Armies are rising up to defend and protect something so clearly wrong, so clearly deplorable that it hates even itself. It's possible that the Danitoreans are good enough, but the rest of the world isn't, and this is just a transitional time for us. Some have speculated that a new prophet will appear soon, to give scriptural basis for all the horrible things Triskelions are doing in the world that effect more than just Danitoreans. To define our role in a future world where it isn't just the Danitoreans we're tormenting."

"You're skirting blasphemy, there."

"You have to admit we're having an impact beyond our desecrated homeland. Otherwise we wouldn't have Celadarian allies and the Tuvali wouldn't care whether we lived or died. Otherwise we'd still be living in blood huts and would never have accepted television or the FÆ into our daily lives."

"There are orthodox Triskelions who do exactly that."

"Who do you think have been at the forefront of the protests? Orthodox Triskelions, of course. Fundamentalists. Extremists."

"Maybe they're right, though. Maybe we shouldn't have let the ways of the world become our ways. Maybe we shouldn't have let ourselves create alliances or accept peace. Maybe we shouldn't presume the right to be passive about what might not even be the real desolation."

"Look, why don't you go talk to them for yourself? Do some research. Pray about it. It's gonna be a while before anything real happens. Don't just accept what the media feeds you and don't take my word for it. Study the scriptures and the facts and form your own opinion. Alright?"

"Maybe I will."

"I hope you do"

. • ● ● • .

"What do you mean, a band of Carpathian goblins has signed a mutual aggression pact with the Knights of Templar fighting on the side of the Danitoreans? Do they even know what this is all about? Goblins are almost as terrible as we are!"

"Sure, and the elves of the Resanctioned Order of the White Guard are about as righteous as they come, which is why they'll be fighting against the goblins if and when any fighting occurs."

"Fighting against the goblins would mean they were fighting against those trying to destroy one of the most despicable species ever to scurry across the face of the Earth. Haven't the White Guard repeatedly implored the Danitoreans to destroy us, over the centuries?"

"Yes. I think they're hoping as much as we are that it never gets to that point. Chances are good. Over a third of all Triskelions have already been rounded up and painlessly destroyed at the hands of Danitoreans, and the only Triskelions still abroad are the bishops trying to prevent an international incident. The rest have returned to the homeland to keep the horrors of our continued existence at a certain minimal level, even as Triskelion population dwindles."

"I've noticed the influx. I also noticed that the protesters outside the clinics haven't been dragged inside and put out of all misery. They won't tell me why, they just keep spouting scripture I already know by heart at me. I'd have thought the protesters would have been the first to go."

"I'm not supposed to say anything about that, but I have overheard a few things, and found a few scriptures that seem to make sense of it. Can I trust you not to go explaining it to the press?"

"Of course you can. I'm hardly a scholar, I doubt they'd listen to my interpretation of scripture, anyway."

"Well you know enough, I think. Think about our lives, our very existence. Think about the way we were created specifically to torment, discourage, and leech off the Danitoreans. Being a thorn in their side is almost literally what we need to do just to survive as Triskelions."

"Yeah, so?"

"So the ones speaking out against the way things are going down are a thorn in the side of the Danitoreans' big push to make the world a better place. If even a single Triskelion stands up not just against the philosophical idea that passively allowing this genocide to happen is a form of choosing death and thus of claiming a right to death, but rather in opposition to Triskelion desolation itself, then clearly we are not the right generation to receive that blessing. If even a single Danitorean prefers to keep this evil in their life rather than to go against the apparent wishes of the protestors, then they clearly are not as good as they need to be to be rid of us. The protesters are fulfilling prophecy and at the same time testing both species' purity of character."

"Plus, it seems clear to me that by protesting on our behalf, they are making sure we -as a species- aren't simply passively accepting genocide. They aren't fighting for our right to live, they're fighting against our right to choose whether we live or die. They're making sure no Triskelion is intentionally depriving the Danitoreans of the depravations we force into their lives. Almost every time I take the time to go talk with them, I feel a strong urge to join their ranks."

"Then you should. Perhaps you can frustrate the Danitoreans more by protesting their kind, peaceful, painless and entirely voluntary campaign of genocide than you can through your normal work. Let the darkness of the spirit lead you along the path toward grossest iniquity."

"But if you're right, and the protesters will be kept alive the longest as a fail-safe, then I'd just be putting off my own death by joining them."

"Be careful, friend. It almost sounds like you're trying to decide how and when you'll die."

"No, I just... I... I guess you're right. I shouldn't be trying to control how soon I die. It isn't up to me. I shouldn't be trying to minimize my own contribution to the pain and darkness in the world. I should be the most Triskelion I can be. I should be the abomination. The parasite. The thorn."

"That's better."

"I think I will join the protests. I can see now how easy it is to slip into an accepting mindset. As though the desolation had already come to pass, and we're just delaying things by not capitulating to the outcome we've been waiting so long for. Just because it's within our reach doesn't mean it's suddenly alright to reach for it. Death is still not ours to take for ourselves."

"Just try not to slip again. I wouldn't want you to slip too far, beyond acceptance and into true opposition."

"Neither would I."

. • ● ● . .

"Are you sure you're capable of that?"

"Does it really matter whether I think I'm capable? I'm Triskelion! It's my duty!"

"But to go into battle? You aren't a warrior."

"None of us are. That isn't the point. The point is to make Danitoreans fight for this victory, to make them put their lives on the line to stand up for what is right."

"But not because you -or any of the other Triskelions fighting with you- believe you have any right to defend yourselves. Right?"

"Of course not! We aren't going into the battle to defend ourselves. We aren't even studying defensive strategies. The heads of the seven armies who will be fighting alongside us are teaching us strictly offensive, aggressive tactics. How to kill, maim, and wound quickly in a battle, and how to get to the heart of the battle so we can be sure we're focusing on the Danitoreans instead of the five armies fighting alongside them. You should come to practice!"

"I'm not so sure I want to be involved in the fight. Actually, I'm not one hundred percent sure it's the right thing to do. Especially with so many other countries and peoples getting involved. Some of them really are fighting for the wrong reasons."

"And they believe they have the right to fight on our behalf. We certainly don't have the right to say what they can and can't do with their own lives. If it weren't for a handful of Triskelions standing up and saying they'd take up arms against the Danitoreans and then negotiating the terms of the battle, at least half a dozen armies would have been fighting and killing each other months ago. Some experts estimate that the Tuvali could have already taken the Danitorean capital by now, if they'd mobilized when they first said they would."

"I still don't understand why they're so eager to stand up for rights we don't have."

"They believe we do. The Celadarians more than the Tuvali, they believe that every form of life is precious and has the right to live, and to choose how they die. The fact that we're an abomination and a plague upon the Earth hasn't escaped their attention, they just don't believe it disqualifies us from what they consider to be basic rights."

"Which is how all this got started. People getting involved where they don't belong. What business is it of theirs whether we die at the hands of the Danitoreans? None."

"It doesn't matter to them. They think they're right. The best Triskelion minds have been trying to explain our position to them, to show them the prophecies and the scriptures and put it all in the context of our way of life and our impact on the world and on the Danitoreans specifically, and they refuse to understand. They see it the way they want to see it, and that's that."

"I just don't know why they'd want to be so willfully ignorant. So self-righteous without regard for the people whose lives they're trying to force their own world view on."

"It doesn't particularly make sense, and they don't gain anything by it, but it's a huge part of why we're dealing with an international incident of this scale. They wanted to stand up for our supposed right to life, and others wanted to stand up for the Danitoreans' right to exterminate the vermin who have been a festering boil on the face of their existence for millennia. The allies of one side pledged assistance along with the enemies of the other. Sworn enemies, political maneuvering and complex trade relationships became involved, and now I'm going to be fighting on the same field as dozens of armies all fighting for dozens of different reasons. Half the people who think they're fighting on 'our side' have never even seen the abomination upon creation that they think they're fighting to preserve."

"They'll see you on the battlefield, though. How many do you suppose will want to switch sides after they get a glimpse of Triskelions?"

"As long as Danitoreans are there, standing up for what they know is right and as long as Triskelions are there making them pay the price for their righteousness, all the other armies that want to kill each other for their own reasons will have to answer to their own gods and their own systems of belief. I'd like to be able to say that we could get through to some of them, that we could do for others what we've been doing for the Danitoreans simply by following through and showing them who we are and why, but that isn't nearly as important as just being a Triskelion and doing it well."

"Good attitude. You've come a long way."

"Studying with and standing by the other protestors has taught me a lot. It's taught me how much I still don't know about the scriptures, and how much I never understood about Triskelion life and Triskelion history. Did you know that there are prophecies that have been interpreted to show that this battle was foretold?"

"Well, we all know there's supposed to be a final reckoning, sure. Armies being raised and the final desolation being hard-fought, but I'd thought that was supposed to be understood symbolically. Like, the Danitoreans would have a hard time reaching a point where they're ready to be rid of us, and would have to fight hard against their habits and traditions and cultural inertia."

"Sure, and that's been going on for a long time, which is why our teachers have been focusing on that sort of interpretation. There are plenty of other ways to read it, and plenty of scriptures the modern interpretation can't explain. Like the part about flashes of blue and flashes of green that hold back all the armies fighting against desolation; it wouldn't make sense if there were only two sides in the fight. I don't know what the flashes will be, but there have to be other armies on the battlefield for that part of the prophecy to come true. Or the stanza describing the final of the twelve prophesied riders coming in on a duhrik to declare the glory of the total desolation of Triskelion abomination. Neither Triskelions nor Danitoreans are allowed by law or custom to desecrate the duhrik with our touch, so the final rider must come from one of the other armies."

"I thought the blue and green were supposed to symbolize the water and the plains separating our cultures from the rest of the world. Wasn't that part of the basis for our general isolationism?"

"To a certain degree, yes, but there are many other places in scripture where we're instructed about our lives being parasitic of the Danitoreans specifically, and admonishing distraction from that central tenet of Triskelion existence. If we look back on the prophecies with the eyes of those in the midst of the final desolation, it's easier to see how the literal translations which have been questioned for so long apply to our actual lives, now."

"You mean, like, the Talgaard mounts?"

"Yeah! They're a great example. Millennia ago, when the prophecies were written, the idea of a mount with teeth like a lion in a face that resembles a human face, wings like an eagle that sound like thunder or like chariots rushing into battle and a tail like a scorpion with a poisonous sting whose poison torments its victims without killing them was bizarre beyond understanding. Then during the escalation of hostilities as more and more parties less and less involved in the desolation itself became entangled in the political imbroglio this has become, the Talgaard pledged to fight and we learned that they ride beasts of exactly that description into all their battles."

"And you'll get to see them with your own eyes. I'm sure it will be amazing to be a part of that, to see the scriptures fulfilled first-hand."

"You could still join us. You haven't been painlessly euthanized, yet, you could still stand up and be a bigger part of fulfilling it, yourself. You haven't missed much of the training, you still have a chance to help ensure that the Danitoreans don't shy away from paying the price for their emancipation from evil."

"I, for one, am not going to change my behavior just because it's the end times. I have a duty, and I've been fulfilling it faithfully my entire life. I don't plan on giving up my Triskelion ideals at the last minute. What I do was what I ought to have been doing ten years ago, it was what I ought to have been doing last year, and it'll still be what I ought to be doing tomorrow. Does anything you're going to be fighting for have value if Triskelions stop being Triskelions at the drop of a hat?"

"Ninety percent of us are already dead. You can't do the work of all Triskelions by yourself."

"But I can continue doing my part of that work until the Danitoreans stop me. And those of us who do keep working, those of us who don't go willingly, we're saying we refuse to make a choice we don't have the right to make. We're saying we refuse to give in, perhaps more than even those of you who'll be forcing Danitoreans to put their life on the line in battle because we'll be proving that we would never stop tormenting, never stop defiling, never stop desecrating until we're destroyed, down to the last Triskelion."

"That's a very sound philosophy."

Self-Serve

"What do you mean, you refuse to train me any longer? I've been your top student for months!"

"Just what I said, Lance. I won't tolerate this kind of behavior in my classroom, and I won't allow my name to be associated with such a vehement practice."

"How is it any different from developing prize hens through animal husbandry or using genetic modifications to infuse your asparagus with a few extra proteins? I've merely developed a menu with the tools, technology and techniques already in broad use in Skythia that captures my essence, clarifies it, and serves it as a four-course meal. That was the assignment, as I understood it."

"You must know that when I asked you to try to develop a menu that captured the essence of who you are as a chef I did not intend for any of my students to go to such bizarre lengths." Chambot tried to explain that the intention of the exercise was to learn about how to evoke an emotional response somewhere between empathy and interpathy by investing oneself emotionally in both the choice of foods and the process of preparation. "A cherished family recipe handed down with the secret ingredient of love and mixed with fond memories and nostalgia that warm your heart as you cook the dish. A style of presentation that speaks to you of home and of familiarity and of comfort, whether through comfort foods mashed together on one big plate or a dozen individual courses laid out in time or in space according to memory and tradition. Learning that the difference between good food and great food isn't in precision measurement, top of the line equipment, cutting edge technologies, and least of all in focus groups and market testing; what makes great food great is the way the chef invests himself fully in it, with love and great care and a full heart."

"I understood all that about the assignment. I've understood all that about great cooking for years. That's why I've longed so long to be a chef, to be able to run my own restaurant. It's something I care deeply about, and something I have very strong feelings about. Your time and attention has meant more to me than I've been able to express, the opportunity of a lifetime to study under someone so in touch with their cooking and their passion, and you've seen that I've been giving my all and doing my best and investing myself fully in everything we've done here." Lance didn't really understand what he'd done wrong, so wasn't sure how to defend himself against this sudden change of attitude. "Even before we met, when I was working with your simulation, learning the basics and getting to know your cooking style and your teaching style, even then, when it was only simulated food made from simulated ingredients, you saw that I did it all with love and great care. You told me that was why you selected my application out of the thousands of remaining applicants. I didn't have the résumé or prior training or any recommendations, you said, but I had heart. Passion. And I've tried to put myself fully into this assignment, more than ever before, so I don't understand what it is I've done wrong, or why you're dismissing me."

Chambot, and the other students who had been trying not to stare as they watched the unfolding altercation, stood dumbfounded for a moment, peering at Lance as though he were some strange, unidentifiable, alien thing, or as though the words he'd said weren't in a language they were fully fluent in and they had to struggle for understanding. "Your main course," said Chambot, holding up the handheld showing Lance's proposed menu. "It's cannibalism."

"Not in any traditional sense."

"You propose serving human flesh to humans. I'm fairly confident that's the traditional understanding of cannibalism."

"That may be true, but none of the things that make it reprehensible are a part of my menu. No murder, no suffering, no chance of BSE or other disease. It's not out of desperation in harsh conditions, and it's certainly not against the will of the meat. I'm literally offering myself up to be eaten. That's more than you'll get out of the cows, pigs, chickens, doves, and frogs on my classmates' menus."

"Only one student has meat from a live animal on their menu, Lance. The vat-grown meat of the others doesn't experience suffering or even death in any meaningful sense."

"Precisely my point. I'm not going to cut chunks out of my own body -well, not more than the biopsies I've already had- I'm growing custom meat in a vat like everyone else. This meat just happens to be cloned from my own cells instead of from a prize winning beef or pigeon."

"Using technology to dress up cannibalism doesn't make it any less terrible. Growing human flesh in vats doesn't change the fact that it's human. The very idea that you think that this is alright is why you're no longer welcome here."

"I suppose we'll just have to see what the public thinks when my restaurant opens. I'm sure I'd have done better with your positive endorsement of my performance, or even just having completed your course, but neither is a prerequisite to my opening a restaurant. Personally, I think Skythians are enlightened enough to have an open mind about the difference between cannibalism as it's thought of and what I'm proposing." Lance really couldn't understand why the entire room full of people seemed so adamant against his idea. It was like the other three courses of his meal didn't even exist, and along with them every day, every meal, every class before this one. "There's not a single original recipe proposed for this assignment by any other student, or in most of the rest of the coursework. Skythia is all about originality, innovation, and following your dreams. Your restaurant's philosophy seemed to be the same. I'm not proposing that a restaurant's patrons murder and eat each other, I'm crafting a four-star dining experience that is literally unmatched in all of creation. What's wrong with that?"

"I'm not going to explain it again, Lance. I just want you out."

"Well, thanks for everything else. It really has been great to be able to work with you. You'll always be welcome in my restaurant, if you change your mind."

. • ● ● • .

"Technically, most of the difference in the dining experience between different cuts of meat has to do with the structure of its growth - we normally only eat Type I skeletal muscle. Genetically all your samples were nearly identical, but we did grow a basic slab from each one for the taste tests you wanted."

"Do we have all the scaffolding I asked for available?"

"Oh, yeah, no problem. All the human musculature is well-mapped for transplants by the medical community, and the bovine musculature is what we're best at here. We grow literally tons of filet mignon at a time. Everything was ready for production yesterday morning, we just needed to know which samples you wanted to run."

"Great. Is the kitchen available now? I could do a quick pan-fry of the samples and get the new growth started on the scaffolds in... half an hour?"

"Yeah, it's all yours. You're the only one with new, untested growth that needs sampling this week, so take your time. All the other people in your class are using tried-and-true standards we always keep a vat or two of online. I'll have a nine-ounce sirloin of each sample transferred to the refrigerator in the kitchen now. Do you know the way?"

"It's through that door, and to the left, right?

"You got it."

Lance didn't think to mention to the meat cloning technician that he was no longer enrolled in Chambot's class, and it didn't really make a difference, procedurally. As an acting citizen of Skythia, he had as much right as anyone else to grow whatever food he wanted, as long as doing so didn't somehow interfere with anyone else's ability to take advantage of the same services.

He walked down the hall to the kitchen and found it to be at least as well-appointed as Chambot's training kitchen had been. He could see through the glass door of the huge fridge that his half-dozen sample sirloin steaks were being deposited on its shelves by robotic arms from somewhere else in the building. He opened the door and pulled the first steak out. The label indicated that it was cloned from his smooth muscle -autonomically controlled musculature, normally only a thin tube or wall of cells that regulated blood pressure, digestion and the like- modern science now allowed him to build a meal around it, if he liked. He got started.

First just the smooth-muscle steak, then all three Type II steaks together -so he could taste them side by side- Lance skillfully prepared and tasted the less likely candidates for his final menu. They were interesting. Strange, even, but not what Lance was looking for. He knew that the technician was right, that he'd probably want to go with Type I skeletal muscle in order to keep his creation in the realm of what people would be able to compare with their entire life's culinary experience. He also had a strong, almost insistent feeling that the right thing to do was to literally put his heart into it, to use cardiac muscle. It had been the most painful and dangerous of the biopsies, but Lance had insisted that they culture his actual heart cells rather than following the instructions in the genome of his every other cell.

When he finally arrived at the point where he had two beautiful, medium-rare steaks in front of him, one from his left psoas major -the muscle of the tenderloin- and one grown from his heart, Lance found that the real conundrum of the day was finally at hand. He ate them slowly, savoring each bite, appreciating the subtle differences in texture and mouthfeel, noticing the variations in each one's aroma and taste and aftertaste and bloodiness and recalling how each one had taken to the heat. Far and away, they were better than the first four. What was possible through science was not always what was best, but if nothing else, science encouraged meaningful experimentation with each possibility to accurately judge what was best. Lance's experimentation had been both influential and inconclusive; four muscle types ruled out, two left standing.

He cleaned up the kitchen and returned to the technician's office. "Is it possible to run the full spectrum of scaffolds for both the cardiac and the Type I skeletal samples?"

"Anything's possible. Which one do you want done first?"

"I need to taste them all before I make up my mind, so it doesn't really matter, I guess."

"Alright. I'll drop the cardiac sample into the scaffolds we already have online, and order a new set of scaffolds for the Type I skeletal." The technician was already busily entering the information into his terminal. "Most of the cardiac will be ready in thirty-six hours. I'll need another four to six hours to get the other set online."

"I'll be back in forty hours, then." Lance looked up the facility's schedule for the kitchen and put himself down for the entire day. "Thanks again for all your help."

"No problem. Can't wait to try the final product."

. • ● ● • .

"I've never outfitted a restaurant quite like this before."

"Do you mean the restaurant design, or my menu?"

"I meant the design. The menu is interesting, but to me it's the way you're going to serve the food that's got my attention."

"I've been to restaurants in Skythia where robots served the food. That's where I got the idea."

"Sure, but they've generally just replaced waiters with automation. A conveyer belt, a robotic serving tray that runs on a wall or ceiling mounted track back and forth to the kitchen, but nothing like this. I'm sure your design will be reproduced soon."

"I can only hope people like it that much. The idea is to create a feeling of intimacy, and to really keep the focus on the food and their dining companions, without distractions from people checking on them at the wrong times, or not checking on them often enough. A fixed menu, with only two options to choose between, coupled with a table that automatically refreshes your drinks and replaces your courses as you finish them, should make for a totally effortless dining experience."

"It's an interesting concept. Putting the kitchen underneath the dining area and serving everything upward through the centers of the tables seems fantastically efficient. Distance from preparation to service is minimized, and the customer's attention is never drawn away from what's right in front of them. If I can get all these robotic limbs working together to pull it off without collision or spillage, anyway."

"Is there another problem?"

"Nothing I can't handle, but I'm going to have to bump my estimate a couple of days. If the tube down the center of the tables could be sixty-five percent larger, I could have it done this afternoon, but then the diameter of the table would be out of spec."

"How far out of spec?"

"Well, in order to give each diner enough room to eat comfortably without worrying about knocking something into the hole..." The technician pulled a diagram up on a large display, showing the table, diners, their individual settings, and the robotic arms serving them, all scaled up to the proposed size. "People on opposite sides of the table would be too far apart. People like to be within arm's reach of each other to feel comfortable and connected, and that would put everyone out of reach."

"I see. Yeah, that destroys the intimacy I'm trying to create. Take whatever time you need." Lance looked over the designs, tried to think of a way to make things easier. In a traditional restaurant setting, a waiter or waitress had all the wide spaces between and around the tables to negotiate the serving of food and the clearing of plates. In his restaurant, it had to be handled in a tube less than half the diameter of the table his guests would be sitting at. "Maybe expand the space as soon as the arms pass the floor, and then traffic would only have to be one way at a time for the three feet between the floor and the top of the table."

"Sure. No reason to keep things confined once they're past the restriction of leaving leg room for people." He tapped away at his terminal, adjusting the specifications of the simulation. "I'm also thinking of doing a side-by-side test comparing 'bots with individual, autonomous control with a single central control for all 'bots. Central control seems better, but I've had some good experiences with unexpected emergent behavior."

"Whatever works best. Don't worry about time. I'm willing to take the time to get things right, regardless of when we open."

"Yet another way your restaurant is different from the others I've worked on in the past."

"I'm sure they cared about quality and getting things just right. Chefs tend to be pretty demanding and very exacting."

"Sure, but they also wanted everything done on a timetable they could set instead of one that I could meet. Always a deadline for a gala opening they'd sent invitations out for before even finding an engineer to build the place for them."

"That's crazy."

"A lot crazier than eating vat-grown human flesh, if you ask me."

"Yet another point we can agree on."

. • ● ● • .

SELF SERVED MEETS FINE DINING
By Bruni Entonago

Whether disgusted by the very idea of the menu, overwhelmed by the elaborate and precise presentation, or frustrated by the lack of options, 'Self Served' is one restaurant that cannot fail to make an impression on you. Recently opened in what some consider the least fashionable part of town, Self Served is situated at street level of Tauer Tower.

If you haven't heard the buzz about head chef Lance's controversial creations, I can tell you first hand that it boils down to little more than hot water under the bridge. I've eaten at restaurants with paint jobs less ethical than Lance's fried appetizers, and if I hadn't had a chance to meet the man myself, I might have suspected that the controversy had been cooked up to build buzz. Read on to find out the truth about what's being done in one of the most revolutionary restaurants to rise to our attention this year.

What you'll notice first, after you've dealt with the weeks-long wait for your reservation to come up, is the unusual interior of the place. Even at midday, Lance keeps the interior of the restaurant dim, and as you walk in your eyes may not have the chance to adjust before you find yourself directed to your table by illuminated colored panels in the floor that will be familiar to every Skythian as a nod to those in our transport hubs.

There is no host or hostess, live or virtual, to greet you. When you walk in, the foyer knows who you are, how many are in your party, and whether your table is ready. A colored circle of light on the floor surrounds the feet of each guest, following you as you wait for your table patiently or wander the room taking in the black on black decor. If you aren't early, there will be no wait at all; a path of matching colored light will extend from your feet into the strange maze of tables that awaits you.

Only the second step on your surreal journey, what you are seeing will not become clear until you are seated at your table and can take in the complete view. Curved sheets of glass extend from floor to ceiling and surround each group's dining experience in a way that evokes the solitary confinement of the cubicle and great distances at the same time. The glass has special optical properties which keep the diners at other tables in focus, though at apparently unbelievable distances. The acoustic properties of these booths and their configuration, designed by acclaimed engineer and sound designer Freidrich Badenhoff, is such that the intimate white noise of the small eatery seems to match the vastness of that visual. It is like eating in an infinite black emptiness, dotted every hundred yards by ætherially glowing groups of guests around each automated table, and otherwise dark and silent.

The tables themselves are a wonder, when you notice them, and a wonder that was designed so you wouldn't. Just as there is no one to greet you when you arrive, there is no one to take your order and no one to serve you your food. Instead, a hole opens up in the middle of the tabletop and all your dishes, drinks, and desserts are delivered to you silently and automatically by what seems to be a many-armed robot.

Choose your seats around the table, and it immediately sets drinks and flatware in front of you, regardless of where around the round table you've chosen to place yourself. During your time at Self Served, you won't have to do anything but eat, drink and be merry, as the table seems to intuitively know when drinks need refills, when each course is completed, and whether you need a clean fork or extra napkins. The meal always progresses at the pace you set, with no waiting for a slow cook or an inattentive waiter, and no fear of your main course arriving before you've finished your salad. (See the pushy staff at the UrucThai downtown, if that's your style, which I reviewed last month.)

Which brings me to the food itself. Lance has tried to control every aspect of the meal, and to design it to his own exacting standard and vision. To this critic, the most obvious misstep of his menu is that he has left no room to maneuver. Everyone gets the same four course meal. Every table, every diner, every day. There is one choice available, between the standard main course and a special one designed to serve two guests and only available by request at the time you make your reservation. Everything else is out of your hands, antipodean to common understanding of 'self serve'. That Lance is satisfied with his choice of dishes, their preparation, and their presentation is clear, and your satisfaction, he says, is up to you.

The first course, everyone's first course, is fried mushrooms. When you read it on the menu, it underwhelms as easily as every other dish when described so simply. Fried mushrooms, salad, steak, and chocolate mousse. What's the big deal, you ask? For the mushrooms, it's presentation.

Before you have the chance to look around, wondering where your wait-staff is to take your order, your table is placing in front of you a scene out of a fantasy novel. On a large, round plate is a færie ring of fried mushrooms, standing guard around a tiny grassy hill that fills the center of the plate. It's almost a shame to disturb the perfect, unique little work of art that's been set before you, but well worth it.

The mushrooms have been grown specifically for this meal, firm yet tender, rich and earthy, with an aftertaste that lingers with you like the memory of a walk in the woods. Almost invisibly battered and fried only long enough to bring forth the fullness of their character without the greasiness commonly associated with the dish, Lance has pushed the boundaries of this bar food into the realm of haute cuisine. Paired with the creamy green dipping sauce whose plentiful and unexpectedly standing wild chives you mistook at first for grass, the heady intensity of the mushrooms can be cut down and, while the complexity then nearly exceeds necessity, the overall experience can be adjusted to suit your palate on a bite by bite basis.

Next up is a sparse salad. Cool, refreshing, cleansing the palate while literally representing an artists' palette of colors on your plate. Another circle, the leaves of the salad are carefully arranged in a spiral on your plate, each leaf a slightly different hue from its neighbors so that the entire arrangement forms a rainbow of color cascading in from the edge of the plate toward the center. No other "greens", no other vegetables, accented with only a light vinaigrette, the salad course is all about the visual.

No dyes, colorants, or tricks of light are used to create this visual splendor, a fact Lance is quite proud of. The new salad "greens" he's had engineered are now available for anyone and everyone to incorporate into their own creations and custom-hued salads are sure to sweep across the menus of restaurants across the city in less obvious ways than Lance's blatant flag waving. Despite such transparency, as part of the whole, this brief break from the complexity, sophistication, and otherwise challenging nature of the rest of the meal provides a welcome balance point upon which the perceived caloric weight of a fried first course and the intellectual weight you will undoubtedly feel as you eat the main course can be leveled.

Which brings you to the part of the review I know most of you have simply skipped to. The main course. First we get one more distraction; for this is the one part of the meal you have any sort of selection power over. Not at the time of your meal, but when you make your reservation, couples have the option of selecting to share a main course designed to serve two rather than eating the default main course.

The default is a simply a steak. A nine ounce filet mignon, wrapped in bacon and cooked medium rare. Always tender, juicy, and flavorful in a way you've never dreamt of, the tenderloin your steak was cut from is grown to the same award-winning standard as all the best filet mignon in Skythia. The difference is that this steak was cloned not by sampling from a prize-winning beef or duhrik, but by sampling cells from the chef himself. The result is both a delightfully different taste and texture for the diner, but a deliciously divisive talking point to spread the word about the restaurant.

The alternative dish, designed with die-hard couples in mind, comes literally from Lance's heart. Cloned from his own cardiac cells to transplant-quality specifications, replicas of Lance's heart are stuffed with a special bacon and mushroom dressing, glazed with honey and baked to glistening perfection. A single, uncut, intact heart is delivered up on a platter in front of its recipients and sliced in half right before your eyes with a laser cutter, revealing all four chambers of the heart brimming with the steaming stuffing. Robotic limbs quickly scoop the stuffing out onto each recipient's plate just in time for the thinly sliced flesh to be arranged neatly over it. The symbolism of sharing a sweet human heart, simply stuffed to the brim with goodness is overpowered only by the spectacle of its presentation.

Each dish has its own strengths, and the two dishes have many similarities as well. The tenderness of the meat is extraordinary, perhaps slightly more that of the heart than that of the filet, but only just. The bacon wrapped around the filet and the bacon in the heart's stuffing tie the two dishes together strongly and at the same time reinforce Lance's personal investment in the meal. The bacon is cloned from samples of his own abdominal muscle and fat, and smoked with a combination of woods he flatly refused to reveal to this critic. The mushrooms in the heart's stuffing, while creating a welcome diversion from the similarities between the dishes, also link the main course back to the appetizer; they are the same mushrooms, repeated.

Either way, after a filling main course your table will quickly and quietly present your dessert. Served in a tall, clear cylinder of glass, the chocolate mousse starts out dark and bitter, well matched to the savory richness of the meat you've just finished. As you eat your way down this shaft of sheer decadence, the mousse becomes creamier, sweeter, and lighter. The final taste is so light and creamy you may wonder how he gets it to stay at the bottom of the dish. The transition from the heaviness of the meat course and its potential psychological and ethical implications to the ease and lightness of being that is embodied by that last bite is perhaps the perfect way to allow people to escape their first encounter at Self Served without having second thoughts about what they've just done.

Overall, aside from the concept of cannibalism and the spectacle of the alternate main course's presentation, the food itself is relatively simple and straightforward. I suspect that repeat diners may actually find the entire thing somewhat disappointing, as the gloss of newness wears off and the glamour of spectacle and exclusivity fade into the background. Lance holds the opposite position, believing that the automation and intimate isolation, coupled with the familiarity and simplicity of the food will draw people back again and again. Rather than trying out every new, innovative restaurant that comes along, he told me, people who appreciate what he has to offer will want to make it a regular part of their routine. He sees the second visit as the point where your attention is free to move past the food, and the apparent isolation from other groups is intended to direct your attention squarely upon the people at your own table. And on conversation.

Which seems true, so far. In order to try both main courses, I've had to return to the restaurant for that second visit, myself. While it was my companion's first venture into that dark, strange place and into what she couldn't keep from calling cannibalism over and over again, I did find that focusing on her face and words was the easiest thing in the world while we were there. The virtual distance kept other guests from distracting me, as did the lack of wait staff, and not being totally alone in the restaurant kept the pressure of forced intimacy and a feeling of isolation at bay. The food was familiar, easy, and its delivery was automatic, effortless, and just as Lance had told me it would be, my attention went right to my companion and it stayed there.

In the end, Self Served is exactly what it says it is; Lance has served himself up to you in a way never before attempted in Skythia. He has created a unique and personal experience that functions on more than one level. Lance puts more of himself into every meal than most chefs dream of, and still he keeps himself and his ego from standing in between you and good food and good company. It is this critic's opinion that Self Served is worth a try. Just be sure to share the experience with someone worth sharing yourself with as deeply as Lance will be sharing himself with you.

Scent of Danger

The bell rang. Three minutes on the clock. Ṟudï's eyes closed. He focused on scent, on odor, on the rhythm of the body and the story it told chemically. He heard the roar of the crowd. He felt the air soft against his skin. Before the split second of his blink had passed, before the resonance of the bell had faded away, Ṟudï had begun his dance.

Round and around and toward and away all at once. The circumference of the cage was significantly larger than the intimate intention for a circle of dancers his specialty stood predicate upon, so Ṟudï had practiced adaptations and variations to suit its scale. Legs flying, his whole body spinning and whirling through the air like a crazed pinwheel, Ṟudï quickly crossed the distance to his opponent. In the time and the intimate air that passed as Ṟudï's leg moved first from the floor into a flowing, wide arc and then into direct contact with the other fighter's face, he scented surprise, dropping confidence, and the remnants of pre-fight preparations.

The blow struck hard and knocked free a distinct metallic, energetic smell R̲udï recognized before the audience caught sight of the tiny glistening red droplets in the bright lights of the arena and he knew he'd drawn first blood well before he'd completed the arc to plant his foot back on the floor and before the sound of the crowd could erupt, filling his ears. Around and around he spun, arms and legs and elbows connecting in a literal whirlwind of motion against a pinned opponent, R̲udï pounded the assault home faster than any reaction other than collapsing could come.

He smelled failure, though not his own. Already, only tens of seconds into the match, R̲udï sensed that his opponent felt outmatched and overpowered. R̲udï sensed the scent of panic. He backed a few lazy, spinning steps away as the challenger clumsily returned to his feet. R̲udï could detect the odor of recklessness rising along with the body of the boxer. He changed his tactic and stance to a more defensive one. He almost immediately smelled the audience's mood turn on him. They wanted the fast kill, the easy win, the red of blood on the ground. R̲udï wanted to fight fair, to pace himself, and to have stamina left to fight another round against a better fighter later that day.

The boxer came at him at a flat charge, dripping the stench of the cornered, defeated animal making a last attempt at survival. R̲udï knew that a solid blow or two to his head with those massive arms behind them would be enough to get knocked out. He spun, dipped, dived, and danced his way between and around the slow throws being leveled at him. R̲udï sprinkled his opponent's body with light blows everywhere he smelled an opening, communicating through such easy contact that the match was already lost. Already lost, but not yet given up. R̲udï smelled a new fury rising up, and a confidence sown in his own overconfidence, and he barely had the time to react before a hard tackle was attempted. A second later R̲udï was yards out of reach and the brute was tumbling along the floor of the cage with all the momentum he'd intended to knock the wind out of the windmill he didn't know how to hit.

R̲udï looked out of the cage for a moment, knowing he was out of harm's way for as long as it took for his increasingly agitated opponent to regain his footing, and saw that over half the match had passed. He considered kicking a man while he was down -it was not against the rules of the tournament- but ended up standing by his good name and good reputation and the good sense to wait until the strong man had farthest to fall. Then he went back into his dance.

R̲udï's ginga was paced precisely to the pugilist's pulsating heart. Punctuating the air with the chemicals in his blood, freed somewhat from the slow passage through the skin and the sweat by the trickle of blood from the nose and a cut above one eye, the boxer set the beat of his own beating. R̲udï allowed himself once more within reach, and this time set himself to the work of completing what he'd begun.

A tap. A step. A slap. A duck. An elbow, hard. A weaving wandering. A cartwheeling kick. A handstand. And then the crunching crack of R̲udï's forehead striking solidly against the other's already broken nose, shattering it.

A howling, yowling, infantile wail of pain.

A sweep of the feet, as the flood of bittersweet ferrous intensity from the eruption of erythrocytes et cetera expanded and overwhelmed other smell, bringing the braying brute crash and bang to the ground. Concussed and blood lossed, he did not move to stand. A quick count. A second bell. Ṟuďi won his round one.

Building; Mark V

After what had happened, Brady felt there was no one he could really talk to besides Paul. After what had happened, Paul didn't want to talk to anyone who reminded him of what he'd done. Brady found himself alone a lot. He found himself alone a lot, but didn't notice how much he talked to himself while alone. Neither did anyone else.

"This is not me. This is not me. I'm not me, not me, not any more." Brady was muttering to himself again while he worked, alone, in his rebuilt lab. "How am I not myself? I'm not myself. Who am I?"

Every last Mark II device had been fed into an incinerator during the cleanup, before the rebuild. No one but Brady knew what had caused everything between his lab and the sky to explode. The recordings, of course, had acquitted him of any involvement. In fact, when the recordings were examined, no explanation at all could be found.

"Not myself. Not myself. Not Mark IV, but not myself any more." Brady was doing the third inventory of his lab that week, obsessively going through every apparatus, every component, every little thing in his lab to be sure of what was there. To be sure of what was real. "Check, check, check. Everything the same. Always the same. Three sonic screwdrivers. Check. Why three? Three. Always three. Check."

The Mark III device, the only Mark III device that had been constructed, had floated harmlessly into the sun after its destruction. No one had even known to examine the records of that device's deployment, intention, or failure. If they had, they'd have found the same lack of an explanation for its failure as they'd found for the shaft of destruction that stopped at Brady's lab. When it had been launched, the Mark III was in working order. When it had reached the sun, it had been little more than scrap metal.

"Four ounces of grey goo. Check. Goo. Check. Nano-material. Four. Four ounces. Sealed. Double-check." Brady stared for a long time at the container of unprogrammed nano-machines. He remembered the Mark IV devices. He remembered that they'd worked. They'd worked on him. They'd worked on him and then they'd stopped. They'd been stopped. "Not myself. Check. Double-check. Double check myself."

Brady did a quick personal inventory. "Fingers, check. Toes, check. Arms, elbows, shoulders, check, check, check. Legs, knees, hips, check, check, check. Body, body, body, body," he patted himself down, stuck in a sort of a stutter, a sort of a loop, "body, body, body, body..." Brady closed his eyes. He took a deep breath. He opened his eyes again. "Body, check. Breath, check." He placed his hands over his chest and felt the rapid thumping away under skin and bone. "Heart, check." His hands moved to his temples, pressing in, trying to feel something that would tell him his mind was intact. "Head..." Brady rubbed his temples hard with his finger tips in a circular motion, feeling the contours of his skull through thin skin. "Head... Check."

Brady's hands moved down to cover his face, he tried to slow his breath, his heart. "Brady, body, check, but am I myself? Am I myself? Am I myself any more?" Brady whispered into his own hands, into the empty room. Brady whispered to no one.

He looked up. "Everything's the same, here. Everything's always the same, here. Nothing's changed. Nothing. Nothing's changed, not since..." His eyes closed again. When he opened them, everything was still exactly where it had been the moment before. "Nothing's changed."

Brady looked around his lab. He'd repeated these same mutterings, these same motions, the same fears and memories he knew no one shared, over and over again. "Something has to change," he finally discovered.

"Something has got to change around here," he announced again to the empty room. To no one. To himself.

"I've got to build something from all this..." He gestured to the lab, to all the parts, the equipment, the various apparatus he'd collected to complete a task that only he remembered he'd accomplished. A task that only he remembered he'd been thwarted from accomplishing. A task that he couldn't embark upon again. "This was meant to build something. All this. For building."

He picked up his handheld. He fingered through, scrolled through the details of the Mark I device, the plans for the Mark II and the Mark III, the software design and hardware template for the tiny Mark IV devices, all built to destroy. Brady tapped away at his handheld for a few moments and while he couldn't actually erase them from the Skythian database, he could hide them from his view, and he did what he could to put that past, all that effort, out of his sight.

"Building. This was meant for building. I should be building. Building."

Brady set down the handheld and moved to a larger terminal. He began putting together a sort of a digital sketch of technical specs for a new device. His hands moved rapidly across the large, touch-sensitive screen of the design terminal. Brady could push the IP of his doomsday devices out of sight in the computer, he could hide it from his view, but he couldn't hide the technologies from his mind. The device he was sketching out on the terminal was technically a marriage of ideas from the Mark I and Mark IV devices, with details and features borrowed from the polished, highly engineered Mark II and Mark III devices. Brady wouldn't have admitted such a thing if one had tried to point it out to him, but he was by himself in the lab, with no one to show him how he was largely recreating what he wanted to put behind him.

Then, as the purpose of the device became ever more clear to him, as Brady pictured in more and more detail what he wanted the device to do, he began searching the Skythian database for suitable IP. Without realizing it, Brady ended up incorporating about half the tech of the machine that Paul had built into his own new creation. Without knowing it, Brady was combining tech from the machine that had caused his own fractured mental state with tech from the devices he hated that he'd unleashed on the world. He was trying to move forward, to do something new, but he was simply recreating history in a new configuration.

At the same time, Brady was doing something which had never been attempted before. When next he looked up from the terminal, it was many hours, nearly days, later. Everything in the lab still looked the same. But when he looked down again at his terminal, he saw the completed plans and specs for the Mark V device. He didn't remember the day and a half he'd spent without moving from that spot. He didn't remember coming up with the idea to design the device. As Brady looked over the plans, the descriptions, all the details worked out, he realized he didn't remember drafting a proposal for the device's use and submitting it to the legislation for approval and a vote. The vote had passed.

. • ● ● • .

"I'm glad to see your work has led you to create something more productive than the doomsday devices you were fighting for the last time we spoke." Colm was at the device's release ceremony as the official representative of Skythia. "This kind of benevolence is exactly the sort of thing that maintains Skythia's positive relationship with other cultures in a way that the destruction of entire urban areas doesn't."

"I've put my old work behind me, Colm." Brady had been given plenty of opportunities to reconstitute his ability to have sane conversations, and conversations with persons other than himself, in the long months since he'd completed the design for the Mark V device. It seemed everyone was suddenly eager to talk to Brady about his work when they found out what the Mark V was supposed to be able to do. "This is just the prototype. I've got some other ideas I'd like to try out as soon as the hubbub from today's test has a chance to die down."

"I'm glad to hear that. If everything goes successfully today, I'm sure you'll get whatever resources and assistance you want for future projects along these lines."

"If my next project goes successfully, I won't have to worry about such things as needing approval or assistance," muttered Brady just before the leader of the Gorlaks refugees walked up to Colm spouting effusive praise and thanks for Skythia's generosity. Brady took the opportunity to slip away into the crowded commerce center. "It won't be long now, and things will get started," he said softly to himself, "and then I can get back to work."

"What was that?" A dirty woman Brady didn't recognize asked him, but he just shook his head and turned away from what must be one of the refugees. He wandered through the crowd, trying to keep quiet, trying to avoid eye contact, to avoid conversation. Finally, after what seemed like longer than necessary, there was an announcement over the PA system warning that the floor was about to become effectively transparent and that guests who experience motion sickness or fear of heights should retire to the upper floors of the commerce center before the Mark V was dropped. Brady breathed a sigh of relief.

The noise level in the room seemed to raise as scientists, politicians, and refugees all felt a growing sense of excited anticipation. A few people retreated up the stairs at either end of the room, and a space cleared around the Mark V device suspended in the center of the room. The display integrated into the floor switched to show the commerce center's exterior, becoming like a huge glass floor that everyone inside was peering down through. A specially-installed iris in the center of the floor of the commerce center opened up, so the Mark V device -about the size of a large beach ball- could be lowered through it. There was a rush of cold air into the room as it opened, and the crowd seemed to involuntarily gasp, and then automatically to cheer all at once as the device began to lower through the floor.

Then, without any kind of announcement or warning, the spherical device was dropped by the robotic claw hand that had been gripping it, and applause erupted all over the room. The iris dilated closed as soon as the robotic claw was back inside, but no one was looking at its reverse journey. Everyone was looking straight down, past their feet, at the device shrinking from view as it fell the hundreds of meters to Earth. When it reached the barren field at the intersection of three nations' borders which had been approved in a devastatingly difficult and lengthy political negotiation for even a few square miles for the Gorlaks to call their own, it seemed at first to disappear.

Everyone in the room seemed to be holding their breath. Even Brady held his breath, unsure whether the device he had apparently designed and submitted in a fugue state would do anything at all. Ten seconds passed. Twenty seconds. Forty seconds. Then, when hope was about to begin to diminish -not even a full minute had passed- someone in the crowd exclaimed "It's working!" Another cheer filled the crowded space of the commerce center's first floor, though Brady wasn't sure any of them had seen anything.

The spell was broken, though, and people were talking, murmuring, pointing, unsure if they were seeing what the others were seeing but excited to see it just the same. After two minutes, everyone could see where the Mark V device was at work; a dark splotch against a barren grey-brown landscape. After five minutes, the splotch had grown to the size of a small village. After ten minutes, the structure of a city's downtown could be seen reaching up into the sky. After fifteen minutes, the foundation for the entire city had been formed, and everyone could see that it had the exact triangular shape that had been agreed upon in the five-party treaty. The commerce center began to lower to the reception area designed for it before the Mark V had built more than an outline for it. In the twenty minutes it took for the commerce center to reach the ground and dock, the Mark V was able to put all but the finishing touches on every house and every office, every road and every train station, every last detail Brady had programmed into its design guideline. Even plant life had been created along with the rest of the city, and the green of lawns, shrubs, and trees were sprouting up all over the city. With permissions granted by the same treaty, roads were extended out from the new city into the territory of each neighboring nation, covering the first half of the distance to the nearest major city in each, along pre-determined routes.

The doors of the commerce center opened up and nearly everyone poured out of it to see for themselves the city that Brady's device had built. Colm sauntered over to Brady, whose attention was already invested in looking over rough plans for a follow-up device on his handheld, and placed a congratulatory hand on his shoulder.

"An entire city, built in under an hour. Amazing work, Brady. Congratulations. The Gorlaks finally have a place of their own to call home. They're forever in your debt."

"I put up a statue of myself in the center of town so they wouldn't forget," joked Brady, not even looking up from his handheld.

The mayor laughed his hearty laugh. "What are you working on now?"

"It's basically the same thing," said Brady, finally looking up from his handheld to meet Colm's eye, "except I want to build another Skythia."

. • ● ● • .

After a small amount of wrangling with the wording of the proposal, Brady was granted permission not only to recreate Skythia for his own personal use, but to take copies of all required AI for the city to function along with all Skythian IP. Simple conditions were added, nothing Brady had a problem with, but it was basically a blanket agreement for a carbon copy of Skythia to be created for a single Skythian citizen's personal use. He had the design for a device to recreate Skythia using a method similar to the Mark V device half done before the Mark V was tested, and though he never entered the sort of fugue state that had allowed him to produce the original design in less than thirty-six hours, he was finished with it before he'd acquired rights to raw material to use it on.

While Brady worked to try to find a nation somewhere on Earth which would allow him to steal sufficient physical resources to build an entire city, he continued building and configuring Mark V devices for whoever needed them. Skythians became jaded about changing the city's route every time another group of refugees wanted a place to live. Brady was able to find locations near the city's normal circuit and worked out a carefully negotiated schedule for deployment that didn't push things too far. Generally, since it was doing so much good for so many people, growing self-sufficient communities that could participate on the global stage out-of-the-box, and building so much good will for Skythia around the world, the Mark V program was well-liked.

The idea that Brady wanted a city all to himself seemed strange to a few people, but they didn't see any harm in it. Paul tried to talk Brady out of it, but Brady knew that all he had to do was bring up Paul's machine to end that conversation, and it ended quickly. Colm wondered what grand plans Brady had for a flying city of his own, but couldn't get any details out of him. Lance had congratulated Brady on the success of the Mark V program and on the approval of his new proposal, but by email - he was too busy developing a second restaurant to take time out to see Brady in person any more.

Eventually, Brady made contact with a nation which actually had a mountain it wanted removed, and would be glad to let Brady's device consume the mountain and fly away with it.

"It ruins the view, you see?" asked King Neergsge'dnama when Brady came to him in person.

Brady looked out from the King's private balcony, high in the royal towers, and took in the view. Brady had never been much for stopping to appreciate landscape. He didn't ever go to the edge of Skythia to see the view. He hadn't studied landscape photography or collected fine landscape paintings. He was not, by far, an expert at judging the relative beauty of any particular view. Yet as he looked out from the King's private balcony, over the breadth of his kingdom and out to the sea, he agreed with the king. "Yeah. I don't know if I've ever seen an ugly mountain before."

"It has been a blight upon the land since the time of my forefathers' forefathers," explained King Neergsge'dnama. "After the time of the treacle wars, when property rights were being negotiated by the seven surviving kingdoms, we were offered the land on which that mountain stands. My forefathers' forefathers were greedy, but foolish. They couldn't turn down the offer of more land, even though they had never seen it. They had a choice between the ground where my people now reside and a much smaller plot of land. They took the larger plot. We've regretted the decision ever since."

"Who got the other plot of land?"

"The Urrelian Precept."

"I've never heard of them."

"They were wiped out. The entire nation sank deeper and deeper into the Earth, eventually being swallowed whole by a portal to a hellish underworld where the Urrelian Precept were tortured and killed one by one at the hands of legions of demons. They were destroyed to the last man, woman, and child, and shown no mercy."

"Oh." Brady wondered if King Neergsge'dnama was aware that his people regretting not being swallowed by a portal to an underworld where they would have been tortured and killed because of this -admittedly ugly- mountain was perhaps not representative of clear thinking.

"We have suffered with this curse for many generations, my friend, and we are eager to see if you can truly save us from our intolerable plight." King Neergsge'dnama was sincere, speaking wholly without sarcasm or humor.

"It's a bit big," said Brady. "Do you have accurate measurements of its volume?"

"Oh, yes, for certain we do. Our wisest scholars have calculated down to the smallest measure of time how long it will take for the mountain to be washed into the sea. Our best minds have measured the weight of this burden upon our people down to the tiniest fraction of a gram. We have thought day and night about this blight on our landscape, praying in earnest that a solution would come." The King slapped an arm around Brady's shoulders excitedly, "and here you are! Truly, my people are blessed by your presence!"

"May I..." Brady hoped he could live up to their expectations. "May I have the measurements?"

"Certainly!" King Neergsge'dnama snapped his royal fingers, and a servant shuffled quickly up to where they were standing, holding out a pillow with a gilded scroll resting on it, eyes averted from his royal presence. King Neergsge'dnama lifted the scroll from the pillow and handed it gingerly into Brady's eager hands. The servant backed away just as quickly as they had approached. The King watched eagerly as Brady read the carefully crafted calligraphy from the glittering scroll.

"Hmmm..." Brady thought out loud as he did some calculations in his head. "Would you..." He drifted off, without finishing his question, still thinking.

"Yes?"

"Oh, err..." Brady looked up from the scroll to King Neergsge'dnama. "Would you be interested in having a new city built where the mountain is, now? I could configure it to your personal specifications. It's just that, there's enough material in the mountain to build my flying city and have about half a mountain left over."

"Half a mountain?"

Brady rolled up the scroll, shoving it roughly into one pocket as he pulled his handheld from another. Since he was out of range of Skythia, it was in offline mode. He held it up to capture an image of the view from the King's private balcony that captured the ugliness of the mountain ruining the view. Then, as King Neergsge'dnama watched, he used image manipulation tools to get rid of the top half of the mountain, by volume. The handheld had captured the image in three dimensions, so he was able to adjust the software model of the mountain, fill in background information by sampling from the colors of the sea and the sky, and show what would be left.

"So, it's half by volume, or about two-thirds of the height that I'll need for my own city. Which will look like this." The image he showed the King was a strange one, with a flattened stump of a mountain dominating the view, almost as strikingly ugly as the mountain was by itself. "Or..." began Brady, quickly pulling up the basic city-modeling software that the Mark V used and procedurally generating the sort of city-on-a-hill that could be effectively carved out of what was left of the mountain after he'd taken what he needed. "You could have a new city standing there, like this," he handed the handheld to King Neergsge'dnama, who used its multi-touch controls to zoom in and out and around the three-dimensional view Brady had mocked up, "where you formerly had just an eyesore."

The King made thinking noises of his own as he considered the option. He furrowed his royal brow.

Brady had another thought. "Ooh! Or, I could redistribute the land. Your nation borders the sea; I could give you more solid ground to call your own. Or a string of islands. Or perhaps a giant statue in the middle of the bay, commemorating your royal likeness? If you're set on having a flat land area there without any development on it, we just need to find something else to do with the mass that's left over."

"A statue, you say?" The King was imagining himself towering over his kingdom, larger than life and remembered forever as The King Who Removed The Mountain. "How tall would it be?"

"Do you mind if I..." Brady reached out for the handheld, and the King was happy to hand it back to him. Brady took a quick capture of King Neergsge'dnama from the front, signaled him to spin around, and captured him from the back as well. He then calculated the volume of stone left in the mountain if leveled to be even with the surrounding area and scaled up the model of the King and dropped it into the model of the bay. Brady had to hold back a laugh when he saw that it was taller than the mountain had been, and twice as ugly. He showed it to the King.

The King seemed to be seriously considering a huge statue of himself towering over his entire country. "More land is more land. We should flatten the mountain and push out the edge of the sea."

Brady felt a sense of relief that he wouldn't be associated with a monstrosity such as a statue of that scale. "Perfect. If you can evacuate your citizens to the countryside, I can actually replicate your current harbor where your new harbor ends up, so no one is displaced, or if you prefer I can land-lock your current harbor and build you a modern one." Brady was tapping away at his handheld, drawing up plans which his modified Mark V would follow to do both parts of the job at once, when he had a thought. "Would you uhh..." He was pretty sure no one had ever been able to ask someone such a thing before, and realized it as he asked the King, "Would you like to design your own coastline?"

King Neergsge'dnama's eyes grew wide, as he realized the extent of the control he was being offered over the future shape of his country. Over his country's future. He was wise enough to know he was not an expert in what makes a coastline. The King's eyes narrowed. He asked, "what is best?"

Brady knew he wasn't an expert, either, but he knew how to find expert information on the FÆ. "I can consult some experts for you, find out what makes the best, most viable and profitable coastline, and design it based on that."

"That sounds advisable," admitted the King.

"Alright, I'll get to work on that, you can decide what you want to do about new construction, and as soon as you can get your people evacuated, we can get rid of that ugly old mountain for you."

Things proceeded rapidly from there, and before the sun set that night, Brady was on board his own flying city, moving slowly away from a country without an ugly mountain ruining the view. Brady was finally alone all day every day, isolated but feeling free, and he never had to talk to anyone but himself unless he wanted to, any more.

Happy Anniversary

They flew West and up and into their futures together, silent but for the sound of the wind whipping his coat and her skirt and the synchronized beating of their hearts.

-Lost and Not Found

They found themselves under the shadow of a thick, white, fluffy ceiling of clouds that blocked the sun from their view, and though they still knew what direction they were traveling in, they moved up through the clouds. It was an amazing thing, to be able to move through the clouds like that. Cold and wet and thick, blocking light and visibility so they couldn't see more than a few feet in any direction, and then suddenly they broke the surface of the clouds and were above them. It was as though they were looking down on an entirely new landscape, just as detailed and interesting as the earth below had been, but white and grey instead of brown and green. They kept traveling in the direction of the sun for a while, until they saw something else there above the clouds, a little to the right of their general direction of travel.

They turned toward it, just an odd speck of dark floating above the landscape of the clouds at first, then growing in size and detail as they approached it. Still a considerable distance away, they could see that whatever it was, it was immense; not someone flying as they were above the clouds - something else. It was almost like a huge mountain poking up through the clouds, but they could see that it was above the clouds and did not extend below them. It was hard to tell until they were almost in reach of it just how big it was, but soon its shapes and details became clearer and they could see exactly what it was.

It was a flying city. They could make out what would have been skyscrapers, had they been built on the ground, but that seemed intensely more impressive raised to this level in the sky. They could see thousands upon thousands of homes and other buildings. The tallest of structures were built at the center. From the looks of it, this floating city housed over a million residents, and was technologically more advanced than the world of the After had been when he had left it. He could see what appeared to be industrial sectors, but there was no apparent pollution pouring out of them, as he had come to expect from such facilities. There was an intricate network of what appeared to be streets throughout the city, but he didn't see any smog over it, nor anything that looked like cars on the narrow streets. He thought perhaps he was too far away to make out such details, but then they were almost on top of the edge of the city, and it still didn't seem like any city he had ever known. This would be quite a different experience from Haven, where only a few thousand lived, and most simply did not desire new technology, whether or not it was available.

He looked over to Tink, and saw that she seemed eager to set down and see what this floating city was all about.

"Let's make a pass over and around the city, get an idea of the best place to set down."

"As long as we stop here, I'm fine with that. This place is amazing! I've seen floating castles before, but never a whole city! I can't wait to meet someone who lives here."

"Me either. But after our first experience with Titana, I'd like to see if we can find something like a City Hall. Someplace we can find out who's in charge and officially introduce ourselves, maybe get a crash course in the city's history instead of just meeting it head on."

"How very logical of you."

"From the looks of it, this is probably a pretty logical town. They may not even believe in magic here."

"Not believe in magic! How absurd!"

"Tink. Think back to the After. They would have disbelieved you right out of existence there! Or worse, disbelieved you into a human. For all we know, this floating city is a technological marvel from the After or someplace like it. I don't want to take any chances with them."

"I wasn't contradicting you. I think it's cute when you get all logical and analytical like that. I can't wait to get you to teach me how to use a comp-you-tor, or whatever you call it."

"They'll probably have plenty of computers here. I'm sure you'll get your chance."

As they had been speaking, they had been flying across the diameter of the city. Most of the structures appeared to have been formed out of some sort of opaque black material. They all appeared as solid as steel, and brand new. He imagined that they looked new because they did not age as other materials were prone to do; this society had found an erosion-proof material and had built everything out of it. He looked forward to learning more about them.

Their architecture was very creative and what he would have considered "futuristic". It was exactly what he imagined the city of the future would look like. As they flew by them, he realized that what had appeared as simple sky scrapers from a distance were complicated structures that rose almost two kilometers above the base of the floating city. Some were single structures that rose almost straight into the sky, but others appeared to be sectional, composed of hundreds of smaller buildings stacked and arranged to form larger constructions like the tiny building blocks he had played with as a child, but on an enormous scale, and most of the blocks were not simple cubes and rectangular extrusions. There was one of these structures that was composed this way, and every other of it's substructures was a sphere; he had no idea how it was held together, but clearly the engineers who had designed it were very advanced. Others were practically sculptural, clearly designed to create a particular look from street level which he couldn't begin to guess at from the sky above.

Just as they were about to pass by the tallest buildings at the center of the circular city, he realized that they had just passed City Hall. He stopped Tink in mid-air and they both spun around to look at it.

"Do you see it?"

"What? Which building are you looking at? The one that's all circles? That one with the weird arms poking out of it a thousand feet in the air? Which one do you mean?"

"City Hall. I found City Hall. Don't you see it?"

"I don't see it."

He flew around behind her and lined his head up along one side of her head and his arm along the other, extending out so he could be sure he was pointing in exactly the right direction for her to see what he was indicating.

"That one. See?"

"I see a really weird-shaped building. How do you know that's City Hall?"

"Those shapes! It spells out City Hall!" He traced out the shapes of each section of the building from top to bottom in the air in front of her:

𐑕
𐑦
𐑑
𐑰
𐑣
𐑷
𐑤

"See? City Hall! In 𐑖𐑱𐑝𐑾𐑯! Don't you remember 𐑖𐑱𐑝𐑾𐑯? In my memory, I mean."

"Is it one of the phonetic alphabets you learned? I don't get it."

"That's okay. Most people only really understand the first alphabet they learned as a child. Shavian is hard on everyone, at first."

"When I was first created, it was before the invention of writing... I'm sorry. But I remember how much you loved the idea of using a phonetic alphabet instead of the one you'd started with! Even if I don't know how to read it yet, I'm sure you'll be a good teacher. You showed me new ways to fly, new ways to paint, new ways to love, I'm sure you won't have trouble teaching me a new way to read. Especially if everyone here uses that alphabet. Do you want to keep looking at the city, or shall we go straight to City Hall?"

"Let's go to City Hall. I'm excited to see if they DO write everything in Shavian."

They angled down into almost a dive and plummeted faster than gravity would have taken them in a free fall to the base of the strangely shaped building that he believed would be City Hall. He guessed that ground level would be the place to enter the building since they appeared to be the only airborne traffic in the entire city, and he was not disappointed to find a huge sign over a wide set of doors that read the same horizontally as the building's entire structure read vertically: 𐑕𐑦𐑑𐑦 𐑣𐑷𐑤. Below that, in equally large block letters it repeated in English: City Hall. They set down, pulled open one of the giant doors that was clear as glass, but light, and stepped inside.

A husky man in a suit that was at the same time professional and made entirely of a shiny plastic material greeted them just inside the door. The man wore a sash that read "𐑥𐑱𐑘𐑼", and held a hand out in greeting.

He took the offered hand and shook it excitedly, saying, "Paul! How are you?"

"I'm doing great. I was glad to learn you survived doomsday."

"It was this one," he said, indicating Tink. "Without her, I wouldn't have made it. But that was a long time ago, and we're here now." He didn't want the conversation to linger on the past, or to the life he'd left behind, so quickly steered the conversation to the present. "You've sure got an amazing city. We weren't sure what sort of reception we might get, but we just had to take a look."

"Oh, you'll be getting the royal treatment from us! Your reputation precedes you two! Not to mention that you just happen to be old friends with the mayor..." Paul turned to face Tink. "Ahh! This must be the lovely Tink!" The Mayor reached out for Tink's hand, and instead of simply shaking it, bowed down to kiss it gently, showing great respect. "Your beauty and grace are well known throughout the region. As soon as you were spotted, rumors began spreading that you might be here to give us a show! Perhaps something from one of his classics, Penelope's monologue, or Chastity's ode to Serenity?"

Tink began to blush from head to toe as he showered her with compliments and praise. "Oh! I hadn't thought! I'm sure I can do something. I don't know how long we'll be here, but what do you think, dear? Penelope? Chastity? Something new? We've only just arrived, you see. We didn't even know we would be coming this way, and ... Oh! It's all so sudden."

"What Tink is trying to say is that she'd be glad to perform something for you, but we'd like to have a proper look around, get acclimated first. I know I'm very interested in the city's history and the background of its technologies. Has the city always been airborne, or did it start on the ground? Or maybe the sea? Has it ever used individual motorized transportation, or is everyone here like you? I didn't see any vehicles on your roadways, and I was wondering how someone would get from one end of the city to the other without it taking half a day. There's so much I want to know, and so much we both want to see. This is just the sort of interesting place we were hoping to explore."

"It is! What a big, complicated place, too! I thought we'd be flying all over the countryside, but this place is so big it might take us a year just to see this one city!"

"More than a year, I think, to see it all. We're already preparing accommodations for you here in the center of town, and you can stay as long as you'd like. If you'd rather live someplace else after you're settled, that's up to you. There's a lot to see in our floating city, and from it; we are not stationary over a single location on the world – we travel far and wide. This opens up opportunities for trade in goods and knowledge that would otherwise be impossible with municipalities on multiple continents and on islands, underwater, and we even come across other flying cities once in a while, most of them daughter cities to this one"

"Your city can build other flying cities?"

"Sure. It's also totally self-sustaining. There's a lot to learn, and we can schedule your orientation for tomorrow. Why don't I take you on a quick stroll through downtown, show you our museum, and then your new home. There will be plenty of time for you to learn about this great city of ours."

"Just two more questions about the city."

Paul was already leading them out, onto the city streets to walk among the tallest of the skyscrapers downtown. "Sure. What do you want to know?"

"First, what's the name of the city?"

The Mayor stopped in his tracks, turned around where he stood, and his face began to take on the shades of pink and red that Tink had shown over her entire body just moments earlier. "Forgive my oversight! I should have started with that, shouldn't I? Yes, well, better late than never. Welcome to Skythia. I'm the Mayor and, as you already know, you can call me Paul."

"Skythia. Interesting. Second, how did you get to be the mayor of a flying city? Last I heard, you were still a car-hating, doomsday-obsessed nobody. Now you drive your own city around the sky and apparently talk about doomsday in the past tense. What happened?"

"That's a long story, most of which I'm sure my wife Mary would rather she got to tell you. It's pretty much the same as your story: I wouldn't have made it without her."

"I look forward to meeting her."

"She's eagerly waiting to meet you both as soon as time permits," Paul said as he led them toward the doors of the museum.

"Oh, is this it? I didn't think it would be so close."

"Yep, it's right here. As much as possible, Skythians like to keep things within walking distance."

"I can see why they elected you mayor," he replied.

Thus they began their tour of Skythia's Great Museum. This museum was not a maze at all, like the old museum of Haven. The entire museum was very modern, with little interactive displays beside every work. They started by showing the basic information about the piece, but could also display a seemingly unending supply of information about the artist or artists including their personal history and information about other pieces by them in the Great Museum and in other museums in Skythia, and the materials used and their origins and traditional uses and what other works used similar materials or materials of similar origin or age, and historical information about the time and place the piece was created in, on and on in more detail that all but the most dedicated scholar was unlikely to use.

The art itself spanned the entirety of history with the first rooms dedicated to pre-historic works. Actual sections of cave walls with early cave paintings having been transplanted to Skythia, and there were examples of the first attempts at pottery and sculpture with a surprising amount of detail about the early men who had created them, as though somehow the information had been extracted through time without disturbing history. The museum gradually progressed across thousands of years of human and non-human history, showcasing important achievements from every cultural group. There was an amazing group of weavings by early elves that depicted a great battle they had won against a rogue army of giants using only simple weapons and the most basic of magic. They actually had genuine Egyptian art and sculptures in better shape than any he had seen in museums in the Darkness or the After, again, as though the works were actually extracted through time from their point of origin without disturbing history.

The museum went on and on through time, showcasing artists they had become aware of during their stay in Haven as well as artists that he had been familiar with from the world of the After. Somehow they had works by Da Vinci he was certain only the Vatican had access to, and they appeared to have somehow extracted the wall on which the Last Supper was painted before the World Wars had nearly destroyed it. He'd had to ask the Mayor about that one.

"This wall can't be the real thing. I've seen the actual wall, still standing, right where it was originally painted. This must be some sort of copy. The real one had been decaying and was damaged in attacks by the Fascists, not in such beautiful condition as this."

"You're part right. In a way, this is a copy. Actually a more accurate description of the technique is that you are looking at a reflection through time of the original, the very moment after it was completed. Like a snapshot through time, made solid and unchanging by the same technology that allows us to reach back through time and see the past with such clarity of detail. When we get to wings showing contemporary works, you'll find that we have similar 'copies' of some of your paintings as well."

"Some would say that making copies of a work without the artist's permission is stealing. Others would say that your copies do not have the same value as the original, no matter how exactly they were made. What do you say?"

"In a way, these are copies, taken without the artists' permission, but without trying to explain a technology I only have a cursory knowledge of myself, these are also the originals. Imagine that we could reach backward through time and remove the artwork from its origin for a tiny fraction of a second, and store that tiny fraction of a second here, so it could be viewed forever. The artist, if he had senses acute enough, might notice his work disappear and reappear for that tiny fraction of a second just as he or she has finished the work, but it is so fast that I dare say neither of you have noticed it of your own works?"

"No... but, how could such a thing work?"

"The way I understand it, once the past has occurred, it is like a solid thing, unchanging. Each tiny fraction of a moment becomes solid and saved in time; the appearance of change in the present is only as we leave behind a trail of static moments in the past and our mind pieces them together into a single, continuous stream. Our engineers have found a way to extract a single instance of a single thing from a single solid moment in the past and freeze it across time in a new location. You really should speak to the engineers about it, though. I'm hardly an expert.."

"I'll certainly have to do that. I'm not sure exactly what to think, and I think we must've lost Tink again, since I know I'm almost lost myself."

They did move on, and they saw the rest of the museum, and just as the Mayor had said, there was a gallery of modern work that included some of their art. It included the painting they had made together of their wedding reception, which made him stop, pull the sack out of his pocket and the original painting out of the sack and hold them side by side, and one over the other. If anything, the 'copy' the museum had looked better than the original, not showing any signs of wear and tear at all. The colors, the textures, the emotion and energy, everything down to the handcrafted stretched canvas made by a friend of theirs in Haven as a wedding present, four feet by nine feet in size, it was all exactly the same. He needed some help getting the original back into the sack, but then they moved on through the rest of the modern works and to the lobby.

"Wait. What about your Future Gallery? Surely you must have a Future Gallery? Even the museum in Haven had a Future Gallery, filled with works that had not yet been created."

"Alas, our technology cannot yet see into the future. We are aware that there are beings, such as the legendary Merlin, who live backward through time, and this tells us that at least for them, the future must be a solid, unchanging thing just as the past is for us. Unfortunately, even the best of our engineers has not been able to determine what it is about such people that causes them to move through time backward, or how to exploit that to extract works from the future. We're actually hoping that someday we'll meet someone with those properties who remembers us solving the conundrum, as that would be like having its certainty guaranteed. Have you ever known someone with that condition yourselves?"

He wasn't sure if it was supposed to be a secret, or what the Skythians would do with the information, so he simply said, "We've met a being or two who lived backward in time, but I don't think they'll be any help here. They knew nothing of your technology when we met them, which means that they wouldn't at any point in our futures. Sorry."

"Someday, I have faith, it will come. Until then, feel free to enjoy all the museums of Skythia; they all use the same technology to deliver the same quality of experience. Just one more benefit of Skythian residence."

"I don't know how long we'll be staying, but we'll certainly not refuse your generosity tonight. Are our accommodations nearby?"

"Everything in Skythia is connected by our transportation system, and it knows where you'll be staying." They walked across the lobby and down to the platform. "The computer systems are much easier to use than the ones you remember. Would you like to try to get there on your own?"

"I think we would. We thank you for your time today. Will we be able to reach you in the future, if we have any other concerns?"

"Most certainly. You two will always have access to me directly." Paul handed him a handheld display, saying, "Use one of these or any console or terminal. Everything in Skythia is connected automatically and wirelessly. It was a pleasure meeting you, Tink, and it was great to get a chance to see you again after all this time. I look forward to seeing you tomorrow after your orientation. Enjoy your night."

"We will."

With that, he and Tink proceeded the remaining distance toward the edge of the platform. Within moments they were together in the privacy of a spherical two-person vehicle, and he found that it seemed to know who they were and that it offered to take them home with a single touch. He turned to Tink who had a look of concern.

"What is it, Tink? Is something the matter?"

"It's just ... this all reminds me of some advanced version of the After. I don't even think they really believe in magic or magical creatures here. If they found out I was a faerie, what would happen? Would I cease to exist? I don't want to disappear because of their ignorance or disbelief. They have all this fancy technology and these massive civil projects and their genius engineers, but do they have real understanding of what living is supposed to be about? Are they happy? Could we be happy here, even for a day or two?"

"Tink, as long as you're by my side and we're safe from harm, I know we'll both be happy. If you don't want to stay here, we can leave right now. Keep flying with the sun and see where it leads us. We aren't tied down, we aren't prisoners, we have no obligation to Skythia. Just say the word, and we'll leave."

"It's not ... I know you want to stay. I know you've been missing technology. You're like a little kid in a candy store, here, and I love that about you. Your enthusiasm, your joy at learning new ideas and experiencing everything you can. You know I share that joy of life, but I worry if it can all be as good as it seems. What if you get stuck here, trying to figure out how to turn their museums to see the future, and you never can? What if being so disconnected from the earth, from nature, what if it saps our strength and life and we become automatons? I don't want to see you go down that path again!"

"I won't, Tink. You won't let me. Don't ever let that happen to me. Promise me that if you see the life start to fade from my eyes, if you see me falling into a rut or forgetting that I love you or that life is for living, promise me that at the very first sign you'll tear me away, take me away, keep me from whatever it is, wherever I am that I'm letting get to me, and kiss me. Promise me you'll never let me lose our love."

"I promise. I promise. Oh, I'll do whatever it takes. I know you love me; I just don't want you to blame me or regret anything we've done or not done. No regrets. I don't want to take you away from something because I think it's changing you only to have you hate me for it."

"I could never hate you, Tink. You're my wife. I'm committed to always love you and stand by you, for the rest of our lives. I know a lot of people in the Darkness, and in the After, and maybe even here in Skythia don't really understand what it means to be committed to someone, what it really means when two people are married, as we are. They think it's just some business contract or a verbal agreement to stick around until things get rough or until someone better comes along. I know it means forever. It means you own my heart. It means there isn't anyone better for me. If I'd ever even considered that there could be someone better for me, or a life better for me without you by my side, not only would you have known about it, but I never would have married you. You're the most important thing to me, my love for you is the biggest part of me, and that will never change." The vehicle split in half to let them out when they had arrived at their destination, but they stayed there, facing each other, tears in both their eyes at the intensity of their conversation, hands in each other's hands, tightly gripping. "We have an advantage over every other couple who ever tried to keep things together, no matter how much they loved each other. We have something that makes it easier for us to understand what the other is thinking and feeling, to know what our motivations and desires are, and to really get into each other's heads and hearts in a way most couples never could. When we kiss," and he leaned in and kissed her for a long moment, and she knew that everything he had been saying was true, that he did want to stay, to learn everything the Skythians had to teach him, but would give it all up without a second thought for her. He knew that she wasn't really afraid of losing him as much as losing the level of constant intimacy and closeness that they had enjoyed in Haven, living and working together most of the time they were there. She worried that the fast-paced always-on lifestyle in Skythia would take so much of his attention that he would hardly have time for her, that her non-technical mind wouldn't be welcome when he met with the engineers, and that she would end up spending more time apart from him than with him. She realized that he had never intended to leave her behind, that he planned to use the city's connectivity and rapid transit to always stay in touch with her when they could not be together physically, and to return to her side at every available opportunity with the speed and ease that had been demonstrated today. She knew that she was his first priority and that she simply had to say the word and he would drop everything and return to her, no matter what, no matter when, and there was nothing for her to worry about. After a long moment kissing that left them both very much more at ease than they had been just a moment before, they separated again, and though he knew she knew what he was about to say, he continued as though he had not stopped at all. "We share everything. That means that there is no communication barrier between us. That means there is nothing I can learn that you can't understand, and vice versa. If you want to come with me to meet the engineers you can, and every time something confuses you or goes over your head or we use jargon you aren't familiar with, which I know won't be very often -you're much smarter than you make yourself out to be- we can just kiss, and all will be resolved. Plus, it means we would get to kiss a lot more than normal in the middle of situations that would otherwise seem..."

She shut him up with another kiss. This time, though they still had that vital sharing of heart and mind and memory, it was all about the kiss. She loved him just as passionately as she had ten years ago when he had returned to Never-never land, and they practically melted together in passion as they sat in the vehicle, kissing as though they had not been married for a day shy of nine years. There was so much love between them, and the next day was to be their nine-year wedding anniversary. When their kiss finally broke, Tink spoke, holding a single thin finger up to his lips to silence him.

"We'll stay here for now. I don't want to spend our entire anniversary traveling to some other town; I want to spend it celebrating with you. After we get a better feel for the town, we can decide how long we want to stay. Right now, let's find a bed and make love all night."

She smiled a wicked grin of a smile at him as her hand slid down and grabbed him just below the knot of his bright orange necktie. She stood up and led him out of the vehicle and into the lobby of the building without looking back at him once or loosening her grip on his tie. She had learned a lot about walking while a resident of Haven, and as she walked across the short distance between where the vehicle had been before it closed and sped away and the elevators, she made a fair amount of spectacle, swinging her hips and walking a very straight line, one foot in front of the other. He didn't even bother pulling his eyes off her swaying hips and her practically sculpted legs peeking out from under her teasingly light skirt.

When they entered the elevator, someone very nearly followed them in, but when they saw Tink turn to him with that look in her eyes that practically dripped sexual energy, the wicked grin still plastered across her face, the interloper quickly exited and found another way up. After the doors closed, she pulled him hard by his tie so his face was right next to hers. She was now definitely floating above the ground, as her eyes were level with his, her nose turned just beside his, her mouth moving in slowly onto his mouth as the elevator automatically delivered them directly to their own accommodations without any need for direction from them. The doors opened and they did not break their passionate embrace as they stumbled into the room.

After a few moments of this passionate stumbling, not wanting to separate, but wanting to find a soft bed, they did eventually have to open their eyes, tear their faces apart and look around.

"It's huge! Are you sure this is the right place? They can't have meant to give us this place. This is a penthouse. That entire wall is a window from floor to ceiling, around the corners! Most of the ceiling is a window on the sky above us, just look up! They've given us an entire floor of a building, and we're high! This is nothing like Trunk's Inn, this can't be right! I wonder how many rooms it has, look at all those doors!" Tink was darting excitedly around the room.

"As long as there's a big soft bed behind one of them, I don't care right now." He began opening doors from one side of the space, and Tink began opening doors from the other, and when they met in the center they looked at each other and said together "Wow." The central door led to the biggest of the bedrooms, though there was another at each end of the space with more of those giant windows facing into it. The central bedroom did not touch any of the outer edge of the building, but it did have a bed twice as big in length and in width as the biggest bed either of them had seen, and when she grabbed him and threw him back onto it, landing right on top of him, they both realized it was not stuffed with anything they'd ever felt before. Their passion was too great to concern themselves with the molecular makeup of their bed for even an instant, and they began what turned into a marathon love-making session the like of which they had had on every anniversary to date, and a couple of times in every month with an 'r' in it's name, and at least three times each in May, June, July, and August. Had they left the bedroom door open, they'd have seen two moons pass overhead, the sun rise and then cross more than half the sky before they even slowed down.

When they did slow down for a few minutes, he called the mayor to make a special request. The communications appeared to include video, so he slipped on a robe before exposing himself to the Mayor. Just in time, too, because the connection went through a lot faster than he'd expected, considering that it was the Mayor, and in the middle of the day.

"First, I want to thank you for these amazing accommodations, Paul."

"It was my pleasure, and the pleasure of the entire community of Skythia, to be able to extend such hospitality to you. Think nothing of it."

"We're going to be staying in for the rest of the day, but I was wondering if you could help us with something."

"Just name it."

"What is the absolute best restaurant in all of Skythia?"

"That would probably have to be Le'Minion. They have the finest cuisine from all the civilizations we have ever encountered. Would you like a table there?"

"Exactly. Today is our nine-year wedding anniversary, and we would like to have dinner at Le'Minion at sunset. Could that be arranged?"

"Absolutely. They will be expecting you at sunset. If you'd like to consider it, their entire menu is available on the internal network." As he said this, Paul must have triggered something from his end, because the Le'Minion menu appeared on the display next to the one that was still showing his smiling face. "I'm glad to hear you two are comfortable. If you should need anything else, don't hesitate to contact me."

"Don't worry, Paul. We won't be interrupting you again today. How about lunch tomorrow, though, maybe with Mary? Whatever your personal favorite lunch spot is."

"Absolutely. Actually, I had your orientation bumped up another day when I was informed this morning that today was your anniversary, so you can do that in the morning and then we can all have lunch together at Self Served." Paul paused for a moment, looked off screen, and muttered, "if I can swing reservations there on such short notice..."

"I thought Le'Minion was the best."

"Oh, they are the best. The absolute best. Just not my personal favorite. Self Served is a little place run by an old friend of mine, and the food there is unlike anything you've ever had. Not the best in Skythia, but different."

"Wait, so you're old friends with the owner, you're the mayor of Skythia, and you aren't sure you can get a table for lunch tomorrow?"

"I'll probably have to make a deal with someone who already has a reservation."

"I'm sure we can wait our turn like anyone else, if you can't. Thanks again for everything. See you tomorrow."

The call was disconnected, and Paul's smiling face disappeared from the screen, replaced with Le'Minion's menu. He didn't really want to consider what they'd be having for dinner quite yet; there was something else he was hungry for just then, and she was coming out of the bathroom with her wings unfolded. Her wings always unfolded during their most passionate lovemaking, and it just seemed to turn them both on more to have her in her totally natural state. Her wings seemed to beat on their own when Tink was at the heights of passion, sometimes even lifting them off the bed unintentionally. Seeing her walk toward him like that, he knew she was still very much aroused, and he hardly remembered to speak before they got back to the task at hand.

"I've just made us some dinner reservations for around sunset."

"Sounds good." She reached him, kissed him, and slipped the robe off his shoulders.

"We've got a few hours, but we'll have to clean up and get dressed."

"Mmmm... clean up. That's a good idea. You've simply got to see the bathtub in here. It puts Trunk's tub to shame." They were pressed together, in each other's arms, almost stuck together with sweat and juices, and began slowly moving as one toward the bathroom.

"I loved that tub. We had a lot of good times in that tub."

"That we did. We're about to have even better times in this one. It's practically a small swimming pool. Want to see how long we can hold our breath?"

"I sure do."

They went into the bathroom and spent the rest of the sunlight hours variously making love and cleaning each other and making love and goofing around and making love again and again in the truly huge bathtub. Eventually they managed to get out of the bath and get dried off and dressed to go out.

"Having magically self-cleaning clothes sure makes things easier. I wonder what we'd be wearing if we had normal clothes?"

"Well, let's see. I think one of these doors was to a closet..." Tink began poking her head behind the doors again until she found the closet. "Aha! We'd be wearing ... well, I know what I'm going to be wearing!"

"What did you find?"

"This!" She had already slipped out of her normal dress and into a more classically styled black evening dress with the deep neck she was used to, but also with no back above her derriere, completely exposing her unfolded and still fluttering wings. The dress flowed down her body as though it had been painted on, all the way down to her ankles, and was slit all the way up her left side to just above the lowest point of the open back. She was absolutely stunning in it. She seemed to literally be glowing, and he loved to be able to see her wings standing out and above and behind her like that as only he had been able to see them during their most passionate moments together; it was like a whole new form of nakedness, of showing more of the woman he loved and accentuating her best features.

"Tink. You. Are. Stunning." He paused as she turned slowly around, still apparently glowing as he had never seen her do at this size before. "You're simply glowing. I love it. Of course, I'll have to find a tuxedo."

"Oh, I couldn't wear this. What would happen when they saw my wings? I'll find something else. Don't even look for a tuxedo. I shouldn't have put it on."

"Don't be silly, Tink! You said yourself that these people probably don't even believe in magic. They couldn't possibly believe in faeries. And they can't disbelieve you, because I believe in you too much for you to ever just disappear. They'll love you, and your wings, you'll see!"

"Do you really think so? I do love this dress. And I love the feeling of being dressed and having my wings out in the open like this. It just makes me feel so alive. Am I really glowing? Do you really think it'll be okay?"

"You tell me." He kissed her gently, longingly on the mouth, just hinting at the passion and anticipation and expectation that the dress made him feel as it exposed her while covering her up at the same time. She knew he truly believed it would be all right, that she would be accepted. She knew that no matter what else happened, she would be safe and protected because of their love. "Now, is there a tuxedo in here I can wear to match you?"

She smiled and pointed, and if the tuxedo had been a snake, it might have bit him, it was right there beside him. He quickly put it on and they were in the elevator and on their way just before the sun began setting over the visible edge of Skythia. Again, they needed not worry about the controls in the elevator, but this time they simply held hands, glancing up and down each other's bodies decked out in formal-wear. It felt so different, so exhilarating to be dressed up differently and a little more special than their normal outfits, and to be in a new place together. They were still basking in the beauty of the long night and day they had spent in the most intimate of embraces, celebrating nine years together and all the years together they were looking forward to. Almost before they knew it they were in a vehicle that knew they had reservations, and then at Le'Minion, and then seated at a table on the outdoor terrace, next to the very outer edge of Skythia, looking out and down at the landscape the city was flying over. They could see the last rays of the sun disappearing over the actual horizon far away below them as they were seated.

"That was amazing. This whole place is amazing. How did you find this place? How did you get us a reservation? They must have us confused with someone else. This can't all be for us. We don't deserve this sort of treatment. Not yet anyway; we just got here!"

"Oh, Tink. You saw how the Mayor treated us yesterday. I asked him to get us a table at the best restaurant in the entire city, and he did. Looks like he got us the best table, too. If the same thing had happened for us in Haven, would it have surprised you?"

"Not really, but we lived there for ten years! We've been here less than two days and they're treating us like celebrities. We haven't even told them whether we plan to stay here at all."

"We are celebrities, Tink. They have our artwork in their Great Museum. Who knows how many other of our works are in their other museums? You know people came from far and wide to meet us in Haven; you had to know that people had heard of us outside of our actual community there. We made a big difference in the lives of almost everyone in that town and asked nothing in return. If you were the Mayor of a city and had the opportunity to welcome two people like us, great artists with a history of immense civil generosity and known to spread joy and well-being like some wonderful kind of disease, where would you stop yourself from accommodating them?"

"I just feel bad taking advantage of their generosity."

"I'm not trying to say that I don't. You know I don't like taking advantage of people any more than you do. We've always had to fight to keep the prices of our works down. We've always done whatever we could so that people would accept our time and hard work as volunteerism, not something that needed to be repaid. We live our lives, do good things out of our joy and happiness and the basic understanding of right from wrong, and because so many people in the world have never seen true love or experienced true community, or seen an example of right living, they don't know how to react. Maybe this entire city has begun to change for the better because of our example. Maybe the generosity they're showing us is representative of their generosity to any strangers that venture into their city. Maybe we'll just have to stay here a long time to feel we've repaid their generosity with generosity of spirit of our own."

"We'd have done that anyway, anywhere we'd stayed. It's just the right thing to do."

"I know that. They may know that. But don't you want to stay here? Think about it. When we showed up here, did they scream in shock at the sight of your wings? Did you shrink to your former size or disappear? Or did they welcome you with acceptance? The maître d' complimented your appearance. What did he say?"

"He said I looked absolutely stunning. That my wings were truly magnificent, and that I was positively glowing. I know. Maybe I'm just being paranoid. I shouldn't be second-guessing everything, should I?"

"No, you should be deciding what you want to eat. We're here for dinner, remember?"

"In a minute. First, I do want to stay. They are nice here, and it does feel really good to be accepted by them, wings and all. I don't know why I was fighting it. They haven't given me any reason to worry. I guess that even though we've been through a couple of big changes together, I'm still not used to it. I was with

Peter for hundreds of years, and nothing ever changes in Never-never land. Changing my home twice in ten years just seems like a lot. I know it's not. I also know I want to have whatever it is he's about to recommend." She turned her glance towards what appeared to be the head chef approaching them.

"Good evening. Welcome to my restaurant, Le'Minion. I am the owner and head chef, Chambot. I trust you are happy with this table?"

"Very happy, thank you. The view is amazing."

"One of the many pleasures you will experience tonight. I have already begun preparing everything for you two; you will be getting the best of the best of what we have to offer, some of it not on our standard menu. Right now, I must return to the kitchen, where I will be personally preparing each course of your meals. Your waiter, Rodney, will be out in just a moment with your appetizers. Of course, if there is anything you desire, do not hesitate to ask. We will do our absolute best to see that you are satisfied tonight."

"Wow, thank you again. We look forward to an amazing meal."

Chambot bowed and quickly disappeared in the direction he had come from.

"I suppose that's why we never saw any menus."

"Actually, the Mayor connected me to their digital menu on the network when we spoke earlier, but I didn't even look at it. I guess that was a good thing. If I'd had a specific meal in mind, I might have been disappointed."

"I doubt you'll be disappointed, no matter what comes out. We're at the best restaurant in an amazingly advanced and culturally sophisticated city, and our dinners are being prepared by the head chef specifically to try to impress us. Every meal we have in Skythia from now on will simply be a disappointment."

"You may be right, Tink. Only the best on our anniversary."

"Happy Anniversary."

"Happy Anniversary."

They raised their glasses and drank to their continued happiness together, and to the future that they were just at the beginning of sharing there in Skythia. Their meal turned out to consist of seven carefully planned courses, each representing a different culture and time period in the history of the world. The foods were rich, but not too heavy. Intensely flavorful, but not overpowering. Each course balanced its elements delicately to their palates, and showed a real artist was at work in the kitchen. The ingredients were all as fresh as any they'd experienced, and seemed all to be selected at just the appropriate moment in development for the purpose to which they were used. The entire experience was enhanced as the two moons rose into view and crawled slowly overhead, illuminating the terrain below and creating an intensely astounding surrounding for their unbelievably amazing meal. At the end of the meal, after they had tasted the most exquisitely crafted sculpture of a desert, and after they'd sipped a light warm cocoa-like drink that seemed to help settle their stomachs after the heavy meal, they found that they were not allowed even to leave a tip in exchange for the meal they'd just had, let alone pay for it.

Chambot came out again to see them off, and while thanking and praising him for the stunning meal, they promised that they would repay him for his generosity someday. He laughed and they left, and were back at their penthouse in no time, and back in bed. This time they just held each other as they'd done their first year together, skin on skin and all tangled up in each other, but without actually making love.

About the Author

Teel is an independent author, artist, creative visionary, blogger, publisher, podcaster, and sometimes filmmaker.

You can find out more about him and his other stories, novels, poetry and more by visiting Modern Evil Press:

http://modernevil.com/

Or email him: teel@modernevil.com

Acknowledgments

More Lost Memories was primarily written during National Novel Writing Month, 2008. It was only with the help and encouragement of my fellow NaNoWriMo participants -especially my wife, Mandy- that I was able to finish writing this book on time. Mandy, incidentally, finished her novel several days before I finished writing these stories. Amber, who for the first time in several years wasn't my official ML, was also quite encouraging, and even offered to help with last-minute proofreading.

Thanks, also, to Heath and Mandy for putting up with my reading the stories aloud to proof read them, to the listeners of the Modern Evil Podcast who also heard a few of these stories before they were edited, and to my father who helped with editing, as well.

Books by Teel McClanahan III

Lost and Not Found
Forget What You Can't Remember
More Lost Memories
Dragons' Truth
The Vintage Collection
Worth 1k --- Volume 1
A collection of poetry instead of pictures
Worth 1k --- Volume 2
Working, eating, pain and longing

Untrue Tales From Beyond Fiction
Recollections of an Alternate Past
-a series-

Book One:
An Introduction To Dodgeball, or
Conception and Induction, or
How To Begin An Apocalypse

Book Two:
The Twofold Invasion, or
Penetration and Destruction, or
How To Make Love With Twins

Book Three:
Escape From Exile, or
Confusion and Contraction, or
How To Get Out Of Hell

Printed in the United States
134508LV00001B/7/P

9 781934 516041